MEG OF HERON'S NECK

By ELIZABETH LADD
Illustrated by Mary Stevens

WILLIAM MORROW & COMPANY
New York, 1961

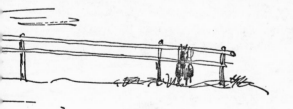

Third Printing, March 1965

Library of Congress Catalog Card Number 61-10769

Contents

CHAPTER 1

Megan Elwell

Megan Elwell sat on the edge of the dock and let her feet dangle over the water, which flowed like smooth green oil around the wharf pilings. On the narrow walk behind her, people pushed and jostled one another—fishermen and workmen, hurrying to their boats, youngsters in shorts and sneakers headed for an afternoon of sailing, and older folks, who were waiting for one of the excursion boats to dock or perhaps just looking at the harbor.

The docks at Summerport were swarming with boats and people on that hot August afternoon. No one gave a second glance at the child, for she was no more ragged and dirty than many of the other children who were darting up and down the runway to the float.

9

Meg leaned far over and watched, as candy wrappers, beer cans, half a sandwich, and an ice-cream cone floated out to tempt the gulls, which had lost all fear of people. On the float, at one side of the main dock, a half-dozen little boys were fishing. They tossed their hooks into the greasy water, got their lines tangled, punched one another in the ribs with their rods, and squabbled among themselves. Meg watched them with a critical eye. "They'll never catch anything," she said to herself.

Megan was ten years old, and like the boys on the float, she wore a thin shirt, blue jeans, and sneakers, very much out at the toes. Her black hair hung down in pigtails, tied at the ends with elastic, and her skin was toasted to a smooth, even tan, without freckles. She had a wide mouth, straight and firm, but her nose wasn't much more than a turned-up button. The dark-brown eyes were narrowed a little from looking so much at sun and sea.

Suddenly Meg leaped to her feet and darted down the runway, which led to the float. A very stout woman, in a white dress and carrying a huge white handbag, was also walking down

the runway, and she completely blocked the
way. Meg dodged under the handbag, nearly
jerking it from the woman's grasp.

"Heavens! What an ill-mannered child!" the
woman exclaimed.

Meg never heard her. She was already on the
float, pushing the little boys aside. "Get out of
the way. My brother's coming in."

The littlest boys obeyed. "Go soak your
head!" one of the larger ones advised Meg.

Megan put her hands on her hips and looked
him up and down. "If you want my brother to
give you a licking, O.K.! If your line gets tan-

gled in the propeller, you'll have to pay for getting it untangled, and that might cost hundreds of dollars. This is my brother's dock, and you haven't any right to use it. He can stop you from fishing here if he wants to."

Not many of these words were true, but they were said with such cold conviction that none of the boys cared to argue. They reeled in their fishlines, and just in time, too, for the sleek white cabin cruiser was already nosing its way gently into the dock. The open cockpit was filled with laughing, gaily dressed people, for the *Dovekie* was one of those excursion boats that carried tourists on hourly sails along the coast.

Meg neatly caught the coiled rope that the captain tossed to her, and looped it around one of the posts. Then she picked up a boat hook that was lying on the dock and helped ease the *Dovekie* in against the float.

The passengers trooped up the three little steps inside the boat and out onto the float. Behind them, Captain Allen Elwell winked at his sister.

Megan thought that her brother was the handsomest man in the world. Allen was almost twenty, tall and slender, with a casual grace in every movement. When he took off his yachting cap, splendid with its gold braid, you saw that his hair was a flaming orange-red. Brown freckles were scattered over his long, straight nose, but his eyes were like Megan's—a dark, velvety brown.

When the last passenger was ashore, Allen hopped onto the dock. "Well done, deck hand," he said, and pulled one of Megan's braids.

"I'm not the deck hand; I'm the mate," Megan answered. "How was the trip?"

"O.K." He turned to the stout lady in white who was approaching them. "Yes, ma'am. This is the Heron's Neck excursion boat. Five dollars, round trip."

"My, that's very high, isn't it?"

"Oh no, ma'am. You'll very nearly have a chartered yacht. It's a two-hour trip. The scenery is wonderful, the weather almost perfect." He gave the lady a charming boyish smile.

"Well," the lady said doubtfully, but she could not help melting a little under the warmth of the smile. "I suppose that is why we're on vacation—to see as much as we can. I think we had better go, John." She raised her voice as she spoke to a rather elderly gentleman who had followed her down onto the float.

"Step right aboard, ma'am, sir." Allen helped the lady aboard. "I'll be back in a minute." To Megan he said, "Watch the ship, mate. I'm going up after a Coke."

Meg jumped down into the cockpit and then went forward toward the cabin. The *Dovekie* didn't really belong to her brother. Allen was just operating it for the summer for the man who owned it. Still, it was easy enough to imagine that this cabin cruiser, finished in warm mahogany, with its glowing brass wheel and all the clever little drawers and lockers, really belonged to them. For an instant, Meg reveled in the delightful dream. Then, with a sense of disloyalty, she thought of their own boat, the chunky little *Sea Mouse*, or "that old tub," as Allen called it. The *Sea Mouse* certainly wasn't beautiful, but it was theirs—or at least it was Allen's. Her brother had told her once that half of the *Sea Mouse*, or of anything else he owned, belonged to her. "Share and share alike," Allen had said.

Allen was the only family she had had since her parents were killed two years ago in an automobile accident. Meg had never known her brother very well until after this tragedy. He was only a half brother. They were both Elwells, but Megan's mother had been her father's second wife, and Allen had gone out on his own while Meg was still a little girl. He had returned as soon as he heard of the death of his father and his stepmother, and since the Elwells didn't seem to have any close relatives, Allen had packed up a few belongings and left his rented apartment, taking his small half sister along with him. Allen's home was the *Sea Mouse,* and for the past two years Megan had lived a free, exciting, and adventurous life.

Meg opened the door to the tiny cabin. From one of the bunks a pair of yellow eyes glowed, and something said, "Purrpt!"

It was a black cat, blacker than the shadows —so black, in fact, that in the half-light his eyes did not seem to belong to any body. As Meg took him up in her arms, he began to bubble and sing noisily, kneading his claws vigorously into her thin shirt.

"There now, Pulsive," Meg said, rubbing his head. "In a few minutes we'll be going out, and you can come on deck."

The cat was kept shut up in the cabin during the time the *Dovekie* was at the dock. This prevented him from running away. But once they were out on the water, Repulsive always came up on deck and sat on a green cushion on top of one of the lockers. "A sea-going cat!" some of the passengers would say in astonishment, but Allen said that ships always had cats. Actually Megan had had him ever since he was a tiny kitten. Allen had brought him home to her one night, buttoned up in the front of his jacket, with only the black whiskers and the baby-blue eyes showing. Repulsive, or Pulsive, as he was known for short, didn't seem to mind living aboard a boat, as long as he was never expected to get into the water.

When Megan came out of the cabin, Allen was already back on the float. He was helping the last two passengers aboard. They were fat old ladies, their arms heavy with bracelets. One of them wore a huge fringed straw hat, which wobbled exactly like a small load of hay. Megan giggled. You certainly saw some funny things around the docks in the summertime.

"Going with us this time?" Allen asked, as he came forward. "Good."

Without being told, Meg hopped onto the dock and cast off the rope. She caught the side rail of the *Dovekie,* scrambled onto the roof of the cabin, and then dropped down to the deck.

The *Dovekie* moved slowly out of the crowded harbor. On all sides there were boats of every size, shape, and color, some lying quietly at their moorings, others being readied for use. Lobster boats, stout and seaworthy, chunky little motorboats, mahogany boats built for speed, with outboards and wide, flaring bows—sailboats not much larger than wooden shoes, but fitted out with sails of crimson or deep blue. Farther out lay the big yachts—floating palaces, with gay awnings stretched over the wide cockpits and all their brass shining.

They passed a lighthouse, which looked like a toy, set among the evergreens. There was little to see along this stretch of shore—only forest, with here and there a house. Repulsive came out of the cabin and seated himself on the green cushion, well beyond the reach of any spray.

"You might hand out some blankets, Meg," Allen said, nodding toward the passengers. "It's cool on the water."

Megan opened the locker that contained the blankets and handed them out to the passengers, who smiled and thanked her. "You're a bright little girl," one of them said kindly. "Is this your daddy's boat?"

"No, my brother's."

"Where do you live in the winter?" one of them asked.

"In town," Megan said, and quickly moved away. Allen had taught her this answer, and he had taught her, too, the trick of avoiding questioners. Some folks might think that life aboard a boat, wandering along the coast, was a rather odd one for a little girl. It was best to keep clear of such people, Allen said.

As it was, the passengers' attention was attracted by something else, for they were coming to their first landing place. No one was to get off the *Dovekie* here, so Allen said, "I'll just swing in and see if anyone wants to get aboard."

There were three ladies huddled in a group

on the slip of the wharf. This was not an easy place to make a landing, for there wasn't any float, as at Summerport, where you could step right into the boat. Instead, there was a wharf with a slip, which was much higher than the *Dovekie*.

Meg had come forward and was watching the slip. "We'll have to back in," Allen said.

He backed the *Dovekie* in skillfully, until the stern was directly under the wharf slip. He shifted the engine into neutral and quickly handed the wheel over to Megan. In a flash, he was back at the stern, helping the ladies aboard. He was in an easy, cheerful mood, as if they had all the time in the world, but Meg knew that it would be only a matter of seconds before the tide swept the *Dovekie* away from the slip. Her fingers tightened around the spokes of the wheel. Why are they so slow? she thought. I could have hopped down in a second.

The ladies were aboard now, and just in time, for the *Dovekie* was edging down sideways against the wharf piling. "Open her up, Meg," Allen called, as he helped the ladies to their seats.

Meg slipped the clutch into gear, and the *Dovekie* moved forward. She stood at the wheel, very proud and straight.

Allen came up and took the wheel. "Ten years from now you can get your captain's paper," he said, laughing.

They were heading straight out into open water now. The land faded away behind them. The dark ridges of the new shore were still very far away. Porpoises leaped out of the sea ahead of them, curving in black half circles. Aroused by their wake, a bell buoy clanged discordantly.

Meg curled up on a bench a little way from the passengers. Here she could watch Allen steer the boat effortlessly, using no more than the tips of his fingers to turn the wheel. She could watch the green-and-white curl of water that fell from the *Dovekie's* bow and see the white jellyfish and the pale-pink ones which were washed back in the wave.

Land was ahead at last—a heavily wooded land, with spruces coming down to the very edge of the water. The *Dovekie* threaded her way in past a lighthouse and through a cluster of lobster boats, as she followed the curve of a

large harbor. Allen pointed out various sights
to his passengers and named the islets that they
passed or the summer estates scattered around
the harbor shore. The cottages looked like dolls'
houses, set on bright-green patches that were
lawns. They had circled around now and were
heading back to Summerport.

Their course lay through a chain of islands,
one behind another, as round as biscuits floating
on the sea. There was one island Meg always
watched for. Allen knew she liked it, so he always took the *Dovekie* in quite close. The shore
was lower than on most of the islands, with little
sand beaches squeezed between the rocks. It
was always a lonely, peaceful place, and wild
ducks would start up out of the coves when they
went by. Megan thought she would like to camp
there some summer, if she could have Allen and
Repulsive along for company.

CHAPTER 2

The *Sea Mouse*

The afternoon sun stood on the very edge of the Summerport mountains, and a golden haze hung over the harbor as the *Dovekie* landed the last of her passengers. Only a few people still lingered on the runways and decks as the mild summer evening approached. The float was deserted by fishermen.

Allen yawned and stretched. "Well, this day is over, and tomorrow is Sunday. Here's some money, Meg. Run uptown and get something to eat. I'll be over to the oil wharf gassing up. Meet me there."

Meg shoved the bills into the pocket of her jeans. "What shall I get?"

Allen rubbed his nose. "Get a steak—two big ones—and bread and lettuce. I guess everything else is aboard the *Mouse*. And tomorrow we'll buy some lobsters. It's either a feast or a famine with us."

Meg ran up the runway and onto the wharf. She was not sorry at being able to run and jump after sitting still for a couple of hours. Boats were nice, but they were certainly limited in space.

The main street of Summerport was almost empty. Most of the people had gone home to supper. The sun still peeped through an opening between two mountains and touched the tops of the brick buildings, turning them a warm, ruddy color, but the street below was already in cool shadows.

Meg made her purchases quickly. They would eat well tonight. What they ate depended a lot on what Allen happened to be earning. With a good job aboard the *Dovekie,* they lived on steak and lobster, but in the winter, when jobs were scarce on the water, they often lived on bread, and on clams which Allen dug himself. Of course, Allen could usually get a job on a scallop dragger. He was quick and strong and "able" with boats, but since Megan had come to live with him, he usually drifted out of the towns in the fall and lived aboard the *Sea Mouse* in some lonely or less frequented cove during the winter. There they existed on what remained of his summer earnings, or from what he could pick up by digging clams or doing a few hours' work at odd jobs, such as repairing a skiff for someone.

Meg had a handful of change left over when her purchases were paid for, and she headed at once for the drugstore soda fountain. It never would have dawned on Meg to save the change, nor would her brother have expected her to do so. Allen freely spent what he had and went without when there was nothing left to spend. After the soda Meg spent the rest of the money on candy bars. She stuffed them into the bag with the groceries and then set out for the dock, where the *Dovekie* was having gasoline pumped into her fuel tanks.

The sun was setting. Even the gulls that wheeled over the almost deserted harbor were slow and sleepy. Allen was ready to cast off by the time Meg reached the dock. "Come on, slow-poke," he said. "I'll drop you and Pulsive off at the *Mouse* and then take the *Dovekie* to her mooring." As Meg hopped aboard he added, "There's a present for you down in the cabin."

Meg put down her bundles and ran into the cabin. Presents were rare in the Elwell family. In the center of the cabin floor stood a good-sized cardboard box, and from it came strange rasping and rustling noises. As she looked, a huge coal-black bill appeared in a crack in the cover and pushed strongly at the cardboard.

Meg stared. "What is it?" she shouted.

"A tame crow," her brother shouted back. "Open the box."

Cautiously Meg untied the string that held the cover down. Out popped a stout black bill surrounded by bristles—much like stiff black whiskers—and then she saw a pair of bright gray eyes, evilly intelligent. The bill flew open, showing an enormous pink throat from which came a terrible clamor. The black cat, Repulsive, fled in terror.

"Goodness!" Meg cried. "You can see all the way to his toes!"

"He's hungry," Allen shouted down to her. "Drop a piece of bread into his mouth."

Meg dug into the loaf of bread, tore off a bit, and dropped it into the pink cavern. The bill closed. "Gobble, gobble," said the crow. Then he was silent and stared at her in a critical fashion.

"We're home now," Allen shouted. "Pack him back into the box and get him aboard the *Mouse*."

"Yar!" shouted the crow, as Meg shoved him down into the box. "Yar!" He tried to bite her.

The *Sea Mouse* didn't have a regular mooring like the *Dovekie* and most of the harbor boats. Allen had permission to keep his boat tied beside part of an old wharf that was falling into ruin and was no longer used. You could board the *Sea Mouse* from the land side, but the wharf was so shaky, with so many broken and missing planks, that it was easier and certainly safer to approach from the water. Now he ran the *Dove-kie* in beside the smaller *Sea Mouse* and un-loaded his passengers and freight.

Meg pushed the crow's box aboard their own boat and dropped the bag of groceries aboard too. She had to drag Repulsive out from under the bunk, where he had hidden after the first squall from the crow. Last of all, Megan herself climbed aboard the *Sea Mouse*.

"All ashore that's going ashore," Allen called, and swung the *Dovekie* clear of the old wharf, heading it out to its mooring in the harbor.

The *Sea Mouse* wasn't much to look at. It was short and chunky and in need of painting— above the water line, anyway. Allen always kept the bottom of the boat tight. There was a cabin on deck, much like the one on the *Dovekie*, but smaller and minus the mahogany and brass. Then you went down a couple of steps to a tiny galley, hardly large enough to turn around in, with a small stove which could burn wood or coal, and with cupboards for the dishes and the few supplies. Beyond the galley there was an inside cabin, really a little bedroom, built in the very bow of the boat. There was a bunk on either wall, and above each bunk a small round porthole let in a ray of light. When you went to sleep at night, you had the whole curve of the ship's prow over your bed.

By the time the clink of oars told that Allen was returning in the skiff, Meg had a fire going in the stove and the food unwrapped. She was starving, and for a moment she thought of eating some of the candy bars. Allen never complained about her eating candy before meals, but the food smelled so good she decided to wait. It was marvelous to be hungry, and know you had plenty of food all around you, waiting to be cooked.

The sunset was ending as Allen came aboard. The glow faded out of the sky, and only the topmost cloud still held a faint flush of color. A pin point of light appeared—the lighthouse on the outer edge of Summerport harbor.

Allen washed briefly in a small enamel basin.

"Got the fire going? Good girl! I'm so hungry I could eat that crow!"

Meg salted and peppered the steaks and then put them on a board well beyond the reach of the cat. Repulsive had regained his courage now that the crow had been put back into his box. Allen set the coffeepot on a corner of the stove. "Feed the cat," he said. "Maybe that will keep him away from those steaks."

Meg opened a can of cat food with the little wall can opener. "Where did you get the crow?" she asked.

"The feller that runs the gas pumps had him. He's a young one. They took him out of the nest this summer and made a pet out of him. But the feller's wife took a dislike to him, and he had to get rid of him. I thought you might like him. But I suspect it was a mistake."

"Why? I *do* like him. And I'm going to name him Crow."

"I don't mean that. A crow can be an unholy nuisance. I don't know what we'll ever do with him, cooped up here aboard the *Mouse*. And the cat hates him already."

Meg put the food down for Repulsive. "You

could build a pen for him. Tomorrow's Sunday, so you won't have to go out on excursions. Pulsive will get used to him. I bet I could train him to do all sorts of tricks."

Allen flipped the steaks into the sizzling frying pan. The hot, sweet smell of cooking meat filled the evening air. Allen yawned, and slapped at a mosquito which had made its way into the galley. "This is the life," he said, looking out over the darkening harbor. "Fog will be in thick enough to cut by morning. You can see it lying out there now. Well, let it. It suits me."

The meal was simple but good. Thick slices of bread, heavy with butter, and plain lettuce, steak, and hot coffee made up the fare. Meg drank coffee with her brother. Allen always let her do it. She fed the crumbs of her steak to Repulsive, who lay heavily across her knees. Darkness closed in, and the light at the end of the harbor vanished under the creeping fog.

A bird called out of the darkness, a harsh and lonely croak. "Blue heron," Allen said in a low voice. "The tide is ebbing. He's looking for his supper."

There were, of course, no electric lights

aboard the *Sea Mouse*. Allen lit the small kerosene lantern and hung it up in the galley. It gave just about enough light for them to find their way around the tiny cubbyhole. They rinsed the dishes off with the hot water that remained in the teakettle. There was never any elaborate dishwashing aboard the *Sea Mouse*.

Meg looked into the box. The crow was asleep, his head under his wing. He grumbled a little at the intrusion and then went back to sleep.

Allen threw himself down on his bunk and lit a cigarette. "I'm not sorry tomorrow's Sunday," he said.

Repulsive climbed onto the bunk with him. The only place the black cat wanted to lie down was on Allen's chest, and he kneaded his claws into the thin shirt. Allen pushed him down, and Pulsive climbed up again—on Allen's face this time. (It was one of the reasons he was named Repulsive.) Allen pushed him away and blew cigarette smoke into his face. Pulsive glared and stalked over to Megan's bunk.

Meg peeped out the cabin doorway. Raw, cold fog, heavy with the scent of the sea, left beads of moisture all over the exposed wood-work. Not a speck of light could be seen in the blackness.

She was glad to creep back into the cozy little inner cabin. She removed her sneakers and sat on the edge of her bunk, wiggling her toes. She wondered if she should wash her feet and then decided against it. There was no more hot water. "I need new sneakers," she told her brother. "There's nothing left of these but the soles."

"You're harder on clothes than any kid I ever saw," Allen growled, but not unkindly. "Next week it'll be Labor Day, and you know what happens after that. This town'll be deader than a doornail. No more excursion work after that."

"Where are we going this fall?" Meg asked.

"Stay in Summerport maybe," her brother answered. "Guess I could get a job on one of the scallop draggers."

Meg sat upright on her bunk, pushing Repulsive aside. "We can't do that, Allen. I'd have to go to school." Her voice was sharp with alarm.

Allen crushed out his cigarette. "Maybe you should go to school," he said uneasily. "After all, how are you ever going to learn to read?"

"No!" Meg cried. "I won't go to school! I can read good now. I can read most all the comic books you bring home. You know what happened the last time I went to school." She began to sniffle loudly.

Allen knew only too well. It had been the fall Meg first came to live aboard the *Sea Mouse*. She had started school then. She had been in the third grade, but something had gone wrong—he wasn't very sure just what it was. Meg had cried all the time and said she hated the school and hated the teacher. Allen never could find out just what happened, but sometimes he wondered if the other children had laughed at her clothes. She had not had any dresses to wear.

It had ended with their leaving town and taking the *Sea Mouse* to a more lonely strip of coast, where few people saw Meg or wondered much about her. If any questions were asked, they moved somewhere else. Meg became adept at avoiding inquisitive folks, and it soon seemed quite usual to her that in the winter life should be lonely and quiet, and that in the summer it should be busy and noisy.

CHAPTER 3

The Visitor

Bang! Bang! Bang!

Megan awoke suddenly and unwound herself from the blanket, which was pulled over her head. The noise came from on deck, so she dressed—she had nothing to do but pull on her shirt and blue jeans—and ran up the step to find out what was going on.

The racket was caused by Allen, who was driving nails. Somewhere he had found a piece of chicken wire, and he was busy building a pen in one corner of the outside cabin. On the cabin floor beside him sat the cardboard box which was Crow's prison, and the box was rocking from side to side. Every now and then a large black beak was thrust out of the hole in the box's cover. Crow was furious to get out, but was prevented from doing so by a string Allen had tied over the top.

"For heaven's sake, get him something to eat," Allen yelled. "Cat food will do."

Meg darted into the galley and got the can she had opened for Repulsive the night before. She yanked the string off the box. It flew open, and out tumbled an indignant and half-starved crow. Instead of being afraid of Megan, he started in pursuit, beating his wings wildly to attract attention, opening his great pink cavern of a mouth, and making as much noise as a foghorn.

Meg used her forefinger to thrust a helping of cat food into the bottomless pit of his throat. After about the fifth helping his mouth was shut for good. He ruffled his feathers, wiped his beak very carefully on Meg's leg, and then went off to inspect Allen's work.

"My goodness, he eats a lot," Meg said. "Have you had any breakfast, Allen?"

"Nope," her brother answered, driving in another staple. "Want to get this pen done first. Watch out for him!" Crow had upset the can of

staples, and seizing one of them in his beak, he started off with it.

Meg had trouble getting the staple away from him. Crow bit her in the finger, and afterward she had to pick up the spilled staples and hold the can for Allen. "It's a good thing he can't fly," she said. "Why can't he fly?"

"His wing feathers seem to be all worn off," her brother said. "Perhaps he was kept in too small a cage, or perhaps he didn't have the right things to eat when he was growing them, so that they never developed right."

Allen finished the pen in a few minutes, and it was just in time, for Crow had now hopped down the steps, and from the galley came the crash of crockery. He had upset the black cat's dish and was now headed for the inner cabin.

"Put him in here," Allen said. "Perhaps we can get breakfast in peace."

It was not easy to put him in. Crow resented being touched, and for his size, he could put up a good fight. When he saw that he was losing the battle, he fell on his back, and thus brought both claws and beak into action. But once he was in his prison, he could not escape, nor was there much that he could damage. He thrust his beak through a mesh in the wire and stood gazing forlornly at all the interesting things beyond his reach.

The Elwells were at a late breakfast when a skiff bumped against the side of the *Sea Mouse*. A man's voice called, "Anyone aboard?"

Allen and Meg stared at one another. A visitor was almost unheard of aboard the *Sea Mouse*. Then Allen wiped his mouth on his sleeve and said quickly, "Probably someone wants me to take the *Dovekie* out special today. See the eggs don't burn, Meg."

Meg moved the frying pan from the front of

the stove, and as Allen went on deck, she decided on another egg for breakfast. She cracked it carefully on the edge of the pan, and as it sizzled in the hot fat, she heard the stranger on deck say, "Thought I'd find you hanging around down here. The old tub looks just the same, Allen."

Megan ate the egg and another piece of toast. She sprinkled sugar and cinnamon over the toast, and then she remembered an orange that was stored away in the locker. It was not until then that she began to feel any curiosity about their guest. Leaving Repulsive to clean out the now cool frying pan, she climbed up the stairway to the deck.

Allen sat upon the high stool, his back leaning against the wheel. The stranger sat on an overturned box in the open cockpit beyond. He was quite a bit older than Allen, and he wasn't much to look at, Meg decided. He had on a pair of very, very dirty dungarees, and there was a rip down the side of his shirt. Even Meg, who thought it a waste of time to wash *every* day, wrinkled her nose at the sight of him. He hadn't shaved for a couple of days, and his coal-black hair needed cutting badly. All in all, he wasn't an attractive sight.

On the other hand, the stranger himself seemed somewhat startled by the sight of a little girl sucking an orange, when her head popped up through the open hatchway. "Well!" he said. "How'd you come by a kid?"

"She's my sister," Allen said rather stiffly. He turned his head toward Meg. "Megan, this is— an acquaintance of mine, Mr. Smalley Blake."

Meg leaned her elbows on the top of the hatchway. She sucked on the orange and stared at Smalley Blake with a pair of critical brown eyes. She didn't bother to say hello.

"Since when have you had a sister?" Mr. Blake asked.

"She's my half sister, if you want to be exact." It was clear that Allen was a little put out. "Dad was married twice, you know."

"Ayeh. I remember they were both killed in a car accident a couple of years ago. How come you've got her?"

Allen shrugged. "We haven't any folks. Dad would never want her put in an orphanage. Meg and I make out all right."

"I should think you'd need a better income than you've got if you're going to bring up a kid. I shouldn't think bumming around the docks would be much of a life for a little girl."

"You think too much," Allen said shortly. "Get us a mug of coffee," he said to Meg. "That's a good girl."

"Him too?" Meg asked pointedly.

"Yes, for him too," Allen said with a sigh. "He's not as bad as he sounds."

The coffee was already hot in the pot. Meg added the waxed paper from the bread to the fire, and this additional heat brought the coffee to a boil. She poured it into two tin mugs and was generous with the canned milk and sugar. When she came on deck again, Smalley Blake was talking about some sort of job that would turn in good pay. Allen listened without comment.

Smalley accepted the coffee and blew on it to cool it. "Good little cook you've got," he said to Allen. "Coffee's not good unless it's boiling."

Meg felt more kindhearted toward him, even though she suspected he was only buttering her up.

"What do you think about it?" Smalley asked, turning to Allen.

"Risky. But probably you're right—there's money in it."

"Will you go in with me?"

"No."

"Why not?"

Allen looked thoughtfully at Meg. "I'm fresh out of coffee, sis," he said. "How about some more?" He had never called her "sis" before.

Meg went down into the galley for the coffee. She took her time, and she kept her ears open. She heard her brother say, "You must see I can't get into anything like that. What would I do with the kid?"

"You going to be stuck with her all your life?" Smalley asked. "Didn't her mother have folks?"

"Ayeh. She had a brother, named Gilbert Duncan. Lot of good he is! He never had any use for us. Said we were a bunch of drifters and never amounted to anything. He was mad as the devil when his sister married Dad. He's got a farm somewhere the other side of the bay— some sort of a chicken farm. Dumb as one of the hens, I bet."

Meg came up with the cup of coffee. Smalley Blake looked at her curiously. "Did you know you had a rich uncle, kid?" he remarked.

A sharp look of annoyance crossed Allen's face. "It'll never do her any good," he said.

Smalley did not seem to notice the annoyance. He thoughtfully ran his fingers over his whiskers. "I was over to Colt's Head not too long ago," he said. "I remember the Duncan farm. He's got a big place there. Got a wife and kid too, I think. He must be worth plenty. Didn't he ever offer to take this kid off your hands?"

"No!" Allen said harshly. "I tell you, he never had any use for an Elwell—not after his sister married one, anyway."

"Did you ever ask him?" Smalley Blake persisted.

"What are you driving at?" Allen demanded. "If you must know, I never asked him. I don't know if he knows that Meg exists. He never kept posted on his sister after she married Dad."

"I was just thinking," Smalley said mildly. "It would be a better life for the kid."

Allen slammed down the coffee mug. His face had turned almost as red as his hair. "I don't know why you're taking such an interest in our affairs. We've got along well enough without anyone's help. I never knew you to be so concerned over a kid," he added.

Smalley Blake said nothing. Meg began to catch her brother's anger. "I hate my uncle," she said, forgetting that it was only a few minutes ago that she first knew she had one. "I wouldn't live on any old farm with a mess of chickens."

"There. You see?" Allen shrugged. "Now let's drop it."

Smalley was willing to drop it. He stayed a

while longer, drank more coffee, talked about boats, and listened while Allen described the *Dovekie*. He even praised Crow and encouraged Meg by telling her about the tricks that he had known tame crows to learn.

At last he yawned, stretched, and said, "Guess I'd better be off." He pulled in his skiff.

"I'm glad you stopped by," Allen said. "If you're going to be hanging around Summerport the next week or so, drop in again."

Smalley steadied the skiff with his left hand. He did not look at Allen. "Sure you won't take me up on the deal?"

"Not the way things stand now," Allen answered.

Smalley Blake pulled away from the *Sea Mouse*, rowing with quick, even strokes. Allen and Meg watched him go. "He's a funny man," Meg said. "I don't think I like him. Smelly Blake would be a better name for him!"

Allen laughed. "He's not a bad guy. I used to see quite a lot of him—once." He fell silent then. Allen loved Meg dearly, and he begrudged her nothing. Just the same, it had been a tame life for him the past two years.

Meg's voice broke in upon his thoughts. "What did he want you to do?"

"Oh, something he had in mind for this winter. Up the coast a ways. Smalley always did have plenty of ideas—not all of them good either. Still, there might be money in it, if we were lucky."

"Are we going to do it?" Meg asked.

"Nope. Too risky with a kid along."

"I'm glad," Meg said. "I don't think I'd like to live with Mr. Smelly Blake."

Allen glanced at his wrist watch. "It's pretty near noon. Guess we'd better take the skiff and see if Bill's over to the car and get us a couple of lobsters for dinner if we can."

For the next few hours the Elwells were so busy with the lobsters that all memory of their visitor was forgotten. But Meg would have liked Smalley Blake even less than she did, and Allen wouldn't have liked him at all, if they could have seen what he was about. He was standing in a public telephone booth, the directory open to *Colt's Head*. His finger ran down the letters. "A ... B ... C ... D ... D ... Duncan!"

CHAPTER 4

Uncle Gilbert

August came to a glorious end. Labor Day was approaching in a few more days, as Allen had said. Summerport would be "as dead as a doornail"—whatever that was. Right now everything was in the last terrible rush. Summer visitors, taking advantage of the last golden days, were swarming aboard the *Dovekie*. Allen's face had grown thinner, his freckles stood out more plainly, and there was less laughter in his brown eyes. Meg didn't wonder at it. It made her tired just to *look* at all the people trooping onto the float.

As she sat now on her old perch above the float, waiting for the *Dovekie* to come in, she thought of what Allen had said last night. "In another week we'll pull out of this town."

She wasn't sorry, even though she liked Sum-

merport well enough. But she was tired of an-
swering questions like, "When will the boat be
in?" and tired of running errands for Cokes and
sandwiches—tired of people. It would be nice
to see nothing but sky and sea gulls again.

She wondered idly what Smalley Blake
would do this winter. They had seen him several
times since his first call. He had picked up a job
at the boat yard at the head of the harbor. Smalley wasn't much of a worker, Allen had remarked, but right now the yard was rushed with
boats being hauled up after the summer's use,
and they weren't fussy about whom they hired.
Meg had seen Smalley once or twice on her way
to the grocery store uptown. He even waved to
her, and she waved back. She didn't hold anything against him—he was Allen's friend.

A man came along the plank walk behind her,
hesitated above the deserted dock, and then
walked on. Meg glanced after him. He was
a tall, well-built middle-aged man—old, he
seemed to Meg—dressed in new khaki-colored
work clothes. She could not quite decide what
he was—not a workman surely. Yet he did not
look like one of the tourists, either.

In a few minutes the stranger returned, and he seemed to notice Meg for the first time. He stopped, leaned over the railing, and looked down at her. "Is this where the boat, the *Dovekie*, stops?" he asked.

He doesn't know much about boats, Meg thought scornfully. "Stops," he'd said, as if the *Dovekie* was a train or something. But after all, business was business. "Yes," she said politely enough. "Did you want to buy a ticket for a cruise? She'll be in to the dock in a few minutes."

The stranger did not answer but stood gazing down at her. He had a strong brown face, with a very square chin and steady dark-blue eyes, which made Meg feel oddly uneasy. "Are you Megan Elwell?" he asked suddenly.

Meg looked up quickly. If the stranger's steady gaze had made her uneasy, his knowledge of her name filled her with downright alarm.

Perhaps the man took her gesture as assent, or perhaps he saw something familiar about the child. He put out his hand, saying, "Megan, I am Gilbert Duncan, your mother's brother."

Meg slipped under the railing and was on

her feet in a flash. Fragments of Allen's words came back to her. "Thinks we're a worthless bunch. Owns a farm. Doesn't know any more than one of his own hens."

She did not take the offered hand but backed well beyond its reach and scowled at her uncle. "What do *you* want?" she asked rudely.

"I've come to take you home with me," the stranger said. He spoke the words kindly, for he really believed that a little girl who had lost both parents and who had no other home than an old boat would be delighted to find an uncle who would take her home with him.

Meg ducked around him before her Uncle Gilbert realized what had happened. She darted up the plank walk toward the town. If her uncle called after her, she did not hear him. Her one thought was to escape. Allen had warned her about people who stole children. This was what her uncle would do—carry her off where Allen would never be able to find her. But she would be too quick for him. She would run uptown and hide, until he got tired of waiting for her or until the *Dovekie* docked. Once Allen got there, she would be safe. Allen would give her so-called uncle a good beating and send him on his way.

Meg dodged around the corner of a building and ran head on into a man.

"Hey, kid! Look out where you're going!" said the indignant voice of Smalley Blake.

Now Megan made her big mistake. She didn't really like Smalley Blake, but he was someone she knew, and he was Allen's friend. He would help her. "Smalley," she cried, "I've got to hide somewhere! There's a man down there who says he's my uncle!"

Smalley stared at her. "Your uncle? Where is he?"

"Down by the float where the *Dovekie* lands."

"The fool, the cursed fool!" Smalley Blake said under his breath. Meg was too excited to notice. "Well," he said more loudly, "we'd better talk with him."

Meg looked at him in horror. "I'm not going back there. Maybe he *is* my uncle, and he'll take me away to that farm, and Allen won't know where I am."

"Do you want him to go to the police?" Smalley Blake asked. "That's what he'll do if he can't find you. No, the smart thing is to go back and have a talk with him. Maybe he's not as bad as you think."

Meg stared at him doubtfully. She didn't want to lay eyes on her uncle again, but Smalley Blake was a grownup. He might know how to handle things better than she did.

"The *Dovekie* is coming in now," Smalley Blake said. "You're not scared of your uncle when your big brother's around, are you?"

"O.K.," Meg said. "But I'm not going down there until she's in." She suited her actions to her words and walked very slowly. She could see that Smalley Blake himself was in a hurry, and it gave her a feeling of satisfaction to see him wait for her to catch up with him.

The *Dovekie* was already at the dock, and the passengers were disembarking when Meg reached the top of the runway and looked down onto the float. Allen was standing on the float. The man who called himself Megan's uncle was standing beside him, and they were talking in low voices. It was impossible to overhear what they said, but Meg, who knew her brother pretty well, could guess what was meant by the quick toss of his red head.

Smalley Blake had already gone down the gangway. He was cursing silently to himself, for he had run into something he hadn't planned on. Duncan *would* have to turn up at just this time, and the kid *would* have to run to him the first thing! Mr. Blake had no desire to have his telephone call revealed, for Allen Elwell had a temper as hot as his hair. But it would not serve Smalley Blake's purpose either, if Allen punched the old farmer in the nose and got mixed up with the police. "What's wrong, Al?" he asked casually, as he approached the two men.

Meg scampered down onto the float and joined them. The passengers had gone up the runway. The float was deserted, except for the little group around the *Dovekie*, for this was the last trip of the day. Meg felt no fear of her uncle, now that both Allen and Smalley Blake were there to defend her. In fact, she looked with some curiosity at the man who thought the Elwells were a worthless bunch.

Gilbert Duncan turned to the newcomer. He

recognized Smalley Blake's voice as the one that
had spoken to him over the telephone, but he
was wise enough not to betray his recognition.
"If you're a friend of this young fellow," he said,
"I'd appreciate it if you'd talk some reason into
him. That little girl back there is my sister's
child. Both her parents are dead, but I didn't
know of their death until some time after it happened. When I made inquiries about the child,
I was told that some of her father's people had
taken her. It was only recently that I learned she
was living around the docks with her half
brother. You must admit it's hardly a decent life
for a child. I intend to take her home with me."

Allen's face was like a thundercloud. "I'm her
brother," he said. "I'm of age, and I've been taking care of her for the past two years. I'll keep
on taking care of her. We never got any help
from you, and we never looked for any."

Gilbert Duncan's lips drew into a thin, tight
line. His eyes were hard and cold. Smalley Blake
said quickly, "No need to have words over it.
Far as I can see, you both want what's best for
the kid. It's likely her uncle can give her more
than you can, Allen."

Gilbert Duncan glanced coldly at the great holes in the knees of Meg's blue jeans. "At least I'll see she has a roof over her head and decent clothes on her back."

Allen flushed beet red. "I know she's not dressed up for a ballroom," he said. "But I'll say one thing. I'll never tell her what you told *your* sister—that I don't want to set eyes on her again!"

It was Gilbert Duncan's turn to flush, but his eyes were as steady as ever, and his voice was calm. "I thought you were a decent fellow, Elwell—only young and hotheaded. I thought you had your little sister's welfare at heart. I can only believe that you did what you thought best, when you failed to notify me of my sister's death and took the child off with you on your wanderings. I can't think that you did this just to spite me. I had hoped that we might come to some agreement over the child, and part as friends. But since you seem intent on causing trouble, I may as well tell you that I have been to see both a lawyer and the Child Welfare Agency. I have taken steps to be appointed temporary guardian of Megan, and I have no doubt but that the welfare agency will be willing to make it permanent."

"But I'm her brother!" Allen shouted.

"Her half brother," Gilbert Duncan corrected him. "Of course you have the right to put in a petition for guardian too. The agency will select the home that offers the best environment."

Allen doubled up his fists. "Get off this float!" he yelled.

"The float is public property," Gilbert Duncan said calmly. "But I will be glad to get off it—with the child."

"You'll take the child over my dead body," Allen answered, and he turned to Smalley Blake.

Smalley spread his hands out in a gesture of despair. "Don't be a fool, Allen," he said. "You can punch him in the nose. But then what? He'll call a cop and have you in jail. Then he'll have the kid anyway. If he's got the papers, like he says, there's nothing you can do."

Allen unclenched his fists. He ran his fingers through his red hair until it stood on end. He looked desperate. "See here," he said to Meg, without meeting her eyes. "You've got to go with

old moneybags, because it looks like he's got the
law on his side. But it won't be for long. Smalley
and I will think up some way to rescue you. I
promise it!"

"But I don't want to go with him!" Meg broke
into a wail. Her brother's surrender had terrified
her. "You said I could always stay with you!"

Allen put his arms around her and hugged
her to him. "I can't help it, honey! He's got the
law on his side, and I haven't! If I refuse, he'll
just bring a cop down here and take you anyway."

Meg clung to her brother, so that he had to
struggle to break free of her embrace. He could
not stand it any longer; he was very nearly in
tears himself. With the last of his self-posses-
sion, he pushed Megan aside and cast off the
Dovekie.

Meg would have scrambled aboard the boat,
but Smalley Blake caught her by the back of her
shirt and held her, while she kicked and strug-
gled. By the time she had bitten him in the finger and got free, the *Dovekie* was headed out of
the harbor. Allen, standing at the wheel, did not
even look back.

Meg burst into sobs. Her brother had abandoned her! She did not understand about guardians or welfare agencies or what Allen had meant by the law's not being on his side or why he should be afraid of a cop. He had just turned her over to her uncle, given her up without so much as a fight, and she felt the bitterness of it to the very bottom of her heart.

A clean handkerchief was put into Meg's hand. She allowed herself the luxury of mopping up her tears. Between sobs, she was aware that the two men were talking.

"I expect you're the one I have to thank for telling me of Megan's whereabouts," her Uncle Gilbert said.

"That's all right," said Smalley Blake in an ingratiating tone. "The dock's no place for a kid to be. Glad I could help you."

A light dawned on Meg. She stopped mopping her eyes and glared at Smalley Blake. "You told him!" she cried. "You told him where I was. Just wait till Allen hears that! He'll—he'll knock your teeth in!"

Smalley Blake looked at her with amused contempt. "He'll never know it, sister."

"I hate you!" Meg screamed. "I always did hate you! Mr. *Smelly* Blake!"

At this point her uncle intervened. He took Meg's hand firmly in his. "Come, Megan. It's late already, and we have a long way to drive. My truck is at the head of the wharf."

Meg tried to pull free. It was astonishing how firmly her uncle held on. "I can't go now. Not without my things."

Gilbert Duncan gave a brief glance at the torn dungarees, the dirty shirt, the toeless sneakers. "There's no point in bothering with your things, Megan. I shall have to buy you all new clothes anyway."

"But there's Pulsive and Crow! I've got to take them! Allen will never remember to feed them." She began to sob again, louder than ever. Several people, who were out for a late-afternoon stroll, stopped and looked curiously at the two men and the sobbing child.

What Gilbert Duncan wanted most of all was to reach his truck and get home. He had been away all day. His wife Laura would be waiting supper for them. He had known that this was not going to be an easy job, but he knew, too, that he was in the right. Still, if it was possible, he would rather not have a scene. He said quickly to Smalley Blake, "Where do they live?"

"I'll show you," Smalley said, and led the way down to the old wharf. "Watch out for the rotten planks," he added, as he guided their way between the many gaping holes down to the place where the *Sea Mouse* was tied.

The three of them boarded the little boat. Crow cawed loudly from his cage. Where was his supper? In the inner cabin the black cat lay asleep on Meg's bunk, for he had not gone along on the *Dovekie* that day.

Meg had thought that once they were aboard the *Sea Mouse,* perhaps in some magic way, everything would change. Maybe Allen would return. Maybe her uncle and Smalley Blake would just vanish—go up in a puff of smoke. But the sad fact was that nothing changed. Allen did not appear. Her uncle did not vanish. He remained, and was remarkably efficient. He found two burlap sacks and some string. Quickly he thrust Repulsive into one sack, Crow into the other. He did not even say anything when Crow bit him. He tied both sacks and handed them to Smalley Blake, who stood by, grinning.

"Have you got your things packed?" he asked Meg, who was standing beside a locker.

"No," she answered.

Uncle Gilbert picked up another sack. He opened the locker and quickly took out the few garments that were in it and stuffed them into the sack.

Meg looked at the little galley for the last time. There was rust on the stove. One of the tin mugs had a dent in it. Everything looked shabby and old. She began to cry once more.

They were on deck again. Smalley Blake carried a sack in each hand, and her uncle carried the third. Meg was still crying when they reached her uncle's truck, which was parked at the head of the dock area. Her uncle threw the sack of clothes into the back of the truck, but he told Smalley to put the animals in the front. "Stop sniffling, Megan!" he said impatiently. "Get in and look after your pets, if you want to keep them!"

He must have given Smalley Blake some money, for as she climbed into the truck, she heard him say, "Thank *you*, sir!" And then, with a touch of irony, he added, "I wish you luck!"

"We'll need it!" Gilbert Duncan said grimly, as he leaned over to lock the truck door on Meg's side. Then the truck roared into life, with a jerk that nearly threw Meg out of the seat.

Meg had no time for a last look at Summerport. Pulsive, bewildered by his imprisonment, stuck his claws through the sack and into her leg. Crow was trying to tear a hole through *his* sack and was having such good success that Meg had to put her feet on top of him. She almost wished he would get out, but then she thought, probably her uncle was mean enough just to throw Crow out into the woods and leave him to starve.

CHAPTER 5

The Farm at Heron's Neck

Gilbert Duncan was not, as Allen Elwell had described him, "an old moneybags." He did own a prosperous farm at Heron's Neck, but the farm prospered because of his own and his wife's hard work and careful judgment. He was not a rich man by any means. It was true, as Allen had said, that he had disapproved of the Elwells and had not been pleased when his sister married one of them. He had never actually said that he didn't want to see her again, but as it happened, he had seen her only once since the marriage, and it had been some time before he had learned of her death.

He had remembered that there was a child, and he had made inquiries, but by that time Megan and her half brother had drifted away, and her uncle assumed that they had joined some of the other Elwells. When he received Smalley Blake's message that his sister's child was running wild around the docks at Summerport, he felt that there was nothing else to do but provide a home for her. His wife Laura agreed with him. They had one child of their own, Christopher, who was twelve. Mrs. Duncan thought that it would be pleasant to have a daughter added to their small family. Her husband, remembering his sister as she had been at Megan's age—a chubby, blond little girl, sweet-tempered and affectionate—had agreed.

But no matter whether he wanted Megan or not, he would have to take her, for he was one of those people with a strong sense of duty. He had not expected Allen to be agreeable—after all, he was an Elwell—so he had gone to the trouble of having the guardianship papers drawn up. It was very unlikely that Allen would ever think about such a thing. In his heart, he believed Allen would be thankful to get rid of the child. If he was disagreeable about it, it was only because it was natural for an Elwell to cause trouble.

Now, as he remembered the unpleasant scene, he was disturbed by the thought that the boy might have been genuinely fond of his sister. He shook off the thought. It was impossible for a child to grow up in those surroundings—in rags and dirt, and exposed to the sort of people Allen Elwell called his friends. He thought with distaste of Smalley Blake.

He could not hide from himself the knowledge that it had been a shock when he first saw the child. Thin, suspicious, with the too-wise dark-brown eyes, there was no Duncan in her—she was Elwell all over. Well, there was no help for it now. Some of the wildness might be from her upbringing—or lack of it. Perhaps Laura could do something with the child.

Meg saw that her uncle had spoken the truth when he said they had a long way to go. They had driven on and on forever. The sun had set; night had come. In the headlights of the truck all the world looked the same. She was very hungry, for her only lunch that day had been an ice-cream cone at the drugstore. The road was hard and bumpy; the sacks with the animals in them kept getting underfoot; and her uncle, wrapped up in his own unpleasant thoughts, had not spoken a word the whole way.

The truck veered off the main road. They came to a house with the porch light turned on. A small collie dog ran out, barking a greeting. The truck stopped, and her uncle spoke at last. "We're home, Megan."

Home! Home was the *Sea Mouse*, tied up snugly against the old wharf, where Allen was boiling lobsters for supper.

The door of the house opened, and a woman called, "Did you bring her, Gil?"

"Yes," Uncle Gilbert answered, and then to Meg he said, "Come. I'll help you with your things."

"I'm not going to get out," Meg said sullenly. "That old dog will chase Pulsive and kill Crow."

"Heather is already used to cats, and she will get used to crows," her uncle said patiently. He opened the door and took out the sack containing the cat. Meg followed, carrying Crow. Under the cover of the darkness, she kicked the dog, who had come up to sniff at her. Heather let out a surprised yelp, but it went unnoticed. Meg wasn't afraid of dogs, but she liked cats better.

The woman came out and helped them with their bundles. "Gil, you look like traveling gypsies!" she said.

Gilbert Duncan sighed, and then he said, "Megan, this is your Aunt Laura." His voice was very firm, as it always was when he spoke to Meg.

"Hello, Megan," her aunt said kindly, and she laid a hand on the child's shoulder.

Meg slipped out from under her touch. She scowled, and she did not say hello. She did not offer to shake hands either. Her uncle shook his head as a signal to his wife.

Aunt Laura was a kindly, sensible woman. She knew that Meg was tired, hungry, and in a strange place, and she did not show much concern, even when she was told what was in the bags. She put them into a side room and closed the door to keep the dog away from them. Then she said, "Supper is waiting. We'll eat first and get things straightened out afterward."

Meg stood in the middle of the strange

kitchen. The walls and ceiling were painted white, and there were red-and-white curtains at the windows. The white-enamel kitchen table was set with dark-red china. It all looked very clean and bright, and Meg sniffed the smell of the waiting supper. She was very, very hungry.

Uncle Gilbert took off his coat and then stroked the dog, Heather, who had pushed her tawny head against his knee. He asked his wife a few questions about the day's activities on the farm, and she answered him briefly while she dished up supper. As he washed up at the sink he asked, "Did Kit see to the broody hens?"

"Kit saw to everything," Aunt Laura answered. "He had supper early, because he had to go to ball practice."

Meg slid into a chair by the table. "Hadn't you better wash your hands first, Megan?" her aunt asked.

Meg's underlip shot out in a pout. "Allen never made me wash."

"You'll feel better if you do," Aunt Laura said kindly. "There's warm water and a towel right here."

It wasn't worth arguing over, with supper so

near. Meg splashed lightly in the water, wiped the dirt off on the towel, and was back at the table in a minute flat.

Supper consisted of baked beans, frankfurters, and hot rolls. Meg was disappointed. Aboard the *Sea Mouse* baked beans were always out of a can and were considered hard-luck fare. True, these were home-baked and looked better than the canned ones. At one side of the table there was a large plate of smooth, rich chocolate cake. Meg reached out a long arm and took a slice.

"You can have the cake *after* you finish your supper, Megan," said Aunt Laura.

Meg stared at her. "Allen lets me eat cake whenever I want to. Ice cream and candy too."

Her aunt made no answer, but Uncle Gilbert was tired, hungry, and worried, and he had heard all he wanted to hear about Allen Elwell. "You're not staying with your brother now, and I don't want him mentioned again this evening," he said angrily.

That did it! There arose before her a vision of the galley aboard the *Sea Mouse*—all snug and cozy, with Allen's red hair glowing, as he bent under the lantern and reached for the coffeepot. Tears began to fall into the beans and over the slice of chocolate cake. Her aunt and uncle pretended not to notice it, but it was a wretched meal for everyone.

Aunt Laura stacked the dishes in the sink without washing them. "We'll get your things tended to first," she said. "And you'll want to go to bed early tonight."

"Allen—" Meg started to say. Then she gave her uncle a bitter look and said no more.

Aunt Laura unwrapped the little bundle of clothes. "Were these all you had?" she asked, looking at the sweater, which the moths had got into, and the patched rubber boots. Then, seeing Meg's face, she added quickly, "We would have had to get you new clothes to start school with, anyway."

Meg started to untie one of the sacks. "What are your pets?" her aunt asked uneasily. Out of the sack popped Repulsive, furious at such treatment, his black fur standing on end and his eyes like golden moons. "Oh, a cat! He's lovely, but I don't know how he'll get along with our cat, Timothy Two. I'd better get him something to eat, and then we'll put him down in the cellar for tonight."

After she had gone for a dish of food for Repulsive, Meg untied the sack containing Crow. Crow was hungry and as furious as Repulsive over the treatment he had received. He stalked across the floor. The wallpaper had big red roses on a white background, and Crow jabbed his beak into one of the roses, pulling a long strip of paper off the wall. Meg sat back on her heels and watched him. It dawned on her that Crow might prove to be more of a nuisance to the Duncans than she herself would.

Aunt Laura, re-entering the room, almost

dropped the dish of dog food. "Good heavens! Get that bird away from my wallpaper!" she cried. When Meg did not move, she tried to push him away with her foot. Crow, who never did like to be pushed, bit her shoe. "He's vicious too," her aunt exclaimed. "Megan, I'm afraid you cannot keep this bird. A cat I can stand, but not this."

"He's my own crow that Allen gave me for a present," Meg shouted. "I won't get rid of him. Allen even built a pen for him."

"Then you should have left him with Allen," her aunt said.

Uncle Gilbert entered the room. "What's wrong now?" he asked wearily. "Oh, it's the crow."

"We'll have to get rid of him. That's final," Aunt Laura said. "I can put up with a lot of things, but not with a crow in the house."

She placed the dish of food in front of Repulsive. Crow was hungry too, and no one seemed inclined to feed him, although he had fluttered his wings and begged for food several times. He did not dare to eat out of the same dish as the cat, so he circled around and gave Pulsive's tail

a good hard pull. Pulsive turned and spat, and the crow, circling him again, seized the edge of the plate in his stout beak. He pulled the plate away from the cat, jerking it along the floor.

Gilbert Duncan laughed in spite of himself. "He's a plucky fellow, and he intends to eat if anyone does. But your aunt is right. We can't have a crow in the house. There's an empty shed I can put him in, until we decide what to do. Give him some supper, Megan, and then I'll take him out."

The cat and the crow were fed at last, and to his great disgust, Repulsive was put in the cellar, while Crow was carried out, grumbling loudly.

Aunt Laura showed Megan her room. It was a small but pleasant upstairs room. Sprays of pussy willows covered the bright-blue wallpaper, and the bed lamp had a blue-silk shade. The white cot bed looked large, compared with the bunk in the *Sea Mouse's* cabin.

"I guess you're tired out," her aunt said, as she

went over the clothes in Meg's bundle and picked out the cleanest shirt and pair of dungarees. "I'll take these downstairs and sew some buttons on them, and you can wear them tomorrow. We must buy you some clothes as soon as possible."

Her aunt hesitated beside the door, wondering if she should kiss the child good night. But Meg sensed her thoughts and drew away from her, so she merely said, "Good night, Megan."

" 'Night," Meg said briefly.

Her aunt went out and softly shut the door. Meg sat down on the edge of the bed and drew up her knees. Aunt Laura was right. She was tired out, and her head ached, and she wanted to cry. Lovely as the room was, she would have traded it for the cabin aboard the *Sea Mouse*, for the curve of the bow over her head, and the thump of Allen's rubber boots.

She saw the shabby little bundle lying on the chair and remembered that Aunt Laura had said they must get her some new clothes. Then she remembered that her aunt had said something about school, too, and she scowled again. She saw very clearly that she was not going to be able to boss her aunt and uncle and make them let her do the things that she had always coaxed Allen into letting her do. Just the same, she wasn't going to stay here long, on this back-country chicken farm, with an aunt and uncle who didn't really want her and who would probably be mean to her.

In her heart, Meg already sensed that these people did not actually want her. She had no understanding of a sense of duty, so she reasoned that Uncle Gilbert had taken her, only because he knew that it would anger Allen. Hadn't Allen as good as said that the Elwells and the Duncans were enemies? And probably Aunt Laura had to do what Uncle Gilbert said.

The thing to do then was to cause so much trouble that the Duncans would be glad to get rid of her. She remembered Aunt Laura's cry when she saw Crow tearing the wallpaper. Perhaps she could get him to destroy other things as well. And Repulsive often lived up to his name. The thought comforted her, as if her animals were allies, bent on helping her. She could do a lot herself, she thought, as she crawled into bed. If she went to school, she would get the lowest rank in the class, so her uncle would be ashamed of her.

In the darkness she missed Repulsive—the weight of his furry body, which was as good as a hot-water bottle, and the sleepy rattle of his purr. She tried to comfort herself by thinking of Allen. As soon as the Duncans found out what a nuisance she was, they would send her back to him. But deep in her mind, there was a thought, which was too painful to touch on. If Allen had really wanted her, would he have given her up so easily? A few tears fell on the pillowcase, and then Meg was asleep.

She awoke in strange darkness. The dream that she was back aboard the *Sea Mouse* was so real that she could smell the sea. Allen had been whistling in the galley beyond. . . . Someone was whistling in the hallway. It grew fainter. It was not her brother, of course, but the sound made her strangely happy. She sighed and went back to sleep.

CHAPTER 6

Kit Duncan

Meg was wide awake when she jumped out of bed the next morning. Bright sunlight fell through an open window, and the collie, Heather, was barking somewhere below. Meg ran to the window and looked out.

There were some tall maple trees to the right of her window. Beyond them she could see a large building—a barn perhaps. But the thing that astonished and delighted her the most, was that beyond the trees and the rolling meadows she had a fine view of the sea.

Last night they had arrived at the farm after dark, and Meg had supposed that it was far inland. Actually the buildings stood on a high ridge, and below them lay an arm of the bay. The water was dancing-blue under the September sun. It was true that the bay was a mile or more away, but the very sight of it lightened Meg's heart.

Between the house and the water were rolling fields, bright with golden St.-John's-wort and the cream-colored disks of Queen Anne's lace. Looking right down into the yard, Meg could see the little collie jumping around. It was hard to feel angry or disagreeable in such a pleasant place. Meg found her clothes, which Aunt Laura had placed on a chair. The holes were all neatly patched and the buttons sewed on.

Aunt Laura was in the kitchen making apple pie. "Good morning, Megan," she said primly. "Your breakfast is ready."

"I'm going to let Pulsive up first," Meg said, running to the cellar door. The black cat was waiting on the top step. "You poor thing!" Meg said. "Did you have to stay in that old cellar all night?"

Breakfast was orange juice, toast, eggs, and a glass of milk. Meg thought about asking for a cooky, but decided against it. She gave Repulsive a lot of toast and eggs—there were plenty of both—and poured out most of her milk into a dish for him.

"Can I have some more toast and eggs for Crow?" Meg asked. "And where is he?"

Her aunt wiped the flour from her hands long enough to get another slice of toast and an egg. "He's in the little shed right next to the hen house. I wouldn't let the cat outdoors now. Heather is out there, and it might be better if they met in the house first."

"All right," Meg said cheerfully, and her aunt sighed with relief. It looked as if the child might settle down in a sensible fashion after all.

Meg went across the driveway and toward a long gray building with rows of windows along its sides. It looked something like a barn, but it was really a two-story hen house. The collie barked a sharp warning, for she was suspicious of Meg. She was a pretty dog, and Meg felt sorry now that she had kicked her. She tried to coax Heather to her with a bit of the toast, but although the collie wagged her tail, she kept her distance.

Meg walked to the end of the gray building, where a door stood open. Much cackling and singing was coming from the open windows. Meg peeped through the door into a large grain room. Bins of grain lined the walls, and there was a stack of it in sacks on the floor itself. The room was shady and cool and had the sweet, musty smell of grain.

A large yellow cat with a white shirt front was sitting on a stack of grain bags. This must be the Timothy Two her aunt had mentioned last night. "Pulsive will soon make hash out of *you*," Meg said aloud.

An inner door opened, and a boy, whistling softly, came out. Meg almost cried out, "Allen!" and yet in the same instant she knew it was not her brother. It was a boy, only a little older than herself, and he was dark-headed, without Allen's flaming hair. But the clear tuneless whistling was so like Allen!

The moment he saw Meg he smiled. "You must be the new one," he said, and it was very hard not to respond to that smile.

Meg managed a scowl, though—a really good one. "Who are you?" she asked in a hostile voice.

"Kit. Kit Duncan."

"Then you're Uncle Gilbert's son."

"That's right," the boy agreed. "That makes us cousins." Heather had come up to him, and he began to stroke the dog's ears.

"I'm not a Duncan. I'm an Elwell," Meg announced.

Kit merely smiled, a secret little smile, and went on rubbing Heather's ears. "I like animals," he said. "Don't you?"

"Yes," Meg admitted. "But where's my tame crow? Your father's done something with him."

"I know where he is," Kit said. "I'll show you." They went out together into the bright morning sunlight.

"I thought this place was way inland," Meg said. "I didn't know it was so near the bay."

"This is called Heron's Neck, because it's a thin little strip of land with water on either side. On this side we're only about a mile from the bay."

"Do you have a boat?" Meg asked hopefully.

Kit shook his head. "Dad never cared much for the water," he explained. "And there isn't much time to fool around the shore. There's a little cove down there with a couple of skiffs in it. I go clamming sometimes, and once in a while I borrow a skiff. Dad doesn't like me to do it, though."

"I lived on a boat for years," Meg said. "A real boat. It belonged to my brother. I know all about boats." She began to describe the *Sea Mouse* to Kit. It sounded more like the *Dovekie* than Allen's tubby little boat, but Kit Duncan would never know the difference.

"Here's your crow," Kit said suddenly. There was no doubt about it. Crow's angry yammer came from the little shed. Meg opened the door, and Crow came up to her in a series of hops, begging to be fed.

"Isn't he black!" Kit exclaimed. "Even his eyes are black! But what makes his feathers so shabby? He hasn't even got a tail. I don't believe he could fly if he wanted to."

"He can't," Meg said. "Allen—he's my brother—said Crow hadn't been fed the right things when he was little—before we got him—by the people who had him first, I mean. So his feathers never developed right."

Meg popped a piece of toast into the wide pink mouth. "Gobble, gobble, gobble," Crow said with satisfaction.

"Now for some nice egg," Meg suggested.

"Yum! Yum! Yum!" Crow said with delight.

"Let me feed him," Kit begged. Crow took the food readily from the boy's hand, but when Kit tried to pick him up, Crow puffed out his feathers and snarled a warning.

"He hates being picked up," Meg warned. "You can scratch his head—he likes that—but if you touch his back, he'll bite."

Crow had now eaten all he wanted, but he had no intention of wasting any food. He stuffed the leftover egg and toast into his mouth until his throat bulged with it. Then, seeing a loose board in the floor of the shed, he hopped over to it and hid the food under the board. Picking up a mouthful of dry leaves that had blown into the shed, he stuffed them into the hole, plugging it nicely.

"It seems too bad to leave him here all alone," Meg said.

"We'll take him back to the grain room," Kit said. "Heather won't touch him, if I tell her not to."

Meg had been gently scratching the crow's head. He loved it, and stretched his neck out, while the white inner eyelids flickered over his eyes. Suddenly she put both hands around him, and before Crow knew what had happened, she had whisked him off the floor. He shrieked at the top of his lungs and hammered on her hands with his huge bill.

"Doesn't he hurt?" Kit asked in amazement.

"Not very much," Meg answered. Actually Crow did hurt—a lot. He had an evil way of pinching with his beak. But she was proud to show Kit how little it bothered her.

Kit sent the collie out of the grain room. "Put him here on this ladder," he said. "It will give him something to perch on." Crow was delighted with the ladder. He could curl his toes over the rounds as if they were the branches of a tree. He sat and looked around him with bright, alert eyes.

"Don't you want to see the hens?" Kit asked Meg. "You can help me pick up the eggs."

Meg felt contemptuous of her uncle, because he earned his living by farming—and poultry farming at that. She remembered Allen had spoken with disgust of anyone who kept hens. So she was surprised to find that the Duncan hens were really beautiful—even to someone who wasn't a farmer. They were big black hens, some of them touched with robin red, and they gathered, singing and cackling, around the children, until you couldn't hear yourself think. They had crimson combs and wattles and bright yellow eyes, and they seemed very tame and delighted to be laying so many fine eggs.

The pens were deep, with clean wood shavings, and some of the hens scratched and dusted, but many of them followed Kit about as if they were good friends of his. Kit gave Meg a pail and showed her how to gather eggs from the nests that lined the wall. "Don't move quickly," he said. "Then they won't be afraid of you."

"Look at how many I've got!" Meg said proudly. The eggs were smooth and warm to the touch, but when she found a hen on the nest, she was afraid to put her hand under it and had to call Kit to help her.

"They break, you know!" Kit warned, when she tumbled an egg into the pail in a hurry. But he was not cross about it.

Meg felt excited and happy. She would help

Kit every day, and soon she would be able to gather more eggs than he did. Perhaps she would even come to like living on a farm and would be glad Kit was her cousin—even if he was a Duncan.

The children were so intent on their work that it wasn't until they were almost back to the grain room that they realized something was terribly wrong. Loud shrieks came from the grain room. Meg almost dropped her bucket of eggs. "That dog! It's after my crow!" she shouted.

Uncle Gilbert was standing in the grain room, holding the crow well away from him, so he couldn't bite him. "What are you doing to Crow?" Meg cried.

Her uncle looked sternly at them. "I told you to keep this bird in the shed. I don't want him in this hen house. Look at what he's done."

He indicated a large hole that had been torn in a bag of grain. As soon as the children had gone, Crow must have hopped off the ladder onto the sack of grain. Using his beak as a dagger, he had hacked a hole through the burlap covering, and mash had spilled out on the floor.

"He only wanted to see what was in it," Meg said.

Her uncle ignored her and turned to his son. "You should know better, Kit, than to bring a crow into a hen house."

Kit flushed red and looked at his feet. Meg felt cross and sullen. All her delight in the farm was spoiled. Uncle Gilbert was a great hand at spoiling things, she thought.

"Take your bird and put him in the shed," her uncle said to her. "Then your aunt wants to see you about getting you some clothes."

Meg took Crow back to the little shed. "Don't you worry," she told him. "Kit and I will smuggle you out when Old Grouchy isn't around. Anyway, I like Kit."

Meg took plenty of time to get back to the house, but by the time she had reached the kitchen door she was in a more cheerful temper. Her aunt had a large mail-order catalogue lying on the kitchen table. It was open to the section on children's clothes, and at the sight of the brightly colored pictures, Meg's spirits rose.

Like most little girls, Meg was fond of pretty dresses, but Allen had never had enough money to buy her many of them. When there was enough money, Allen had let her buy whatever she wished. Since Meg chose clothes for color rather than quality, they never lasted long, and she would soon be wearing dungarees and her old sweater again.

"I don't know if we'll be able to get into town before school starts," Aunt Laura said, flourishing her tape measure, "so I'm going to order you some clothes from the catalogue."

Meg was already thumbing through the pages. "I'd just love this yellow coat," she cried, and then turning to another page, she said, "Look at that darling blue bonnet! Can I get that too, Aunt Laura?"

"What you need most of all are shoes, socks, and underwear," her aunt said sharply. "There isn't a thing in the whole bundle of clothes that's fit for you to wear to school." Aunt Laura's voice was both tired and angry. It would take most of the morning to check over Meg's wardrobe and make out a list of the things needed. Besides, a whole new outfit would make a good-sized dent in Aunt Laura's budget. She had thought that surely some of Meg's clothes would be usable.

Meg grew sulky and disappointed once more. It was clear to her that she wasn't going to get any of the clothes that she wanted. The things she picked out were either too highly priced, or else they were what her aunt called "not service-able." At first her aunt tried to explain why a pale-yellow coat of fine cashmere was not a good buy for a farm girl, who needed a warm coat that would be stout enough to stand the rough-and-tumble of a school bus five days a week. Then Aunt Laura grew short of time and temper and simply took Meg's measurements and jotted down numbers without bothering to consult her.

At last there was a long and expensive-looking list of shoes, overshoes, stockings, a winter coat and hat, a half-dozen washable cotton dresses, and many other things. Meg scowled at the list. What was the sense in having new clothes if you couldn't have what you wanted?

Aunt Laura folded the list with a sigh. "I guess that finishes it. It's time to start dinner, too," she added, glancing at the kitchen clock.

"I'm hungry," Meg said. "Can I have a cooky?"

"Not now. It will spoil your dinner."

This was the last straw. Her uncle made her keep Crow shut up in a shed, her aunt ordered her a new outfit without buying anything she wanted, she was going to have to go to school after all, and now she couldn't even have a cooky when she was hungry.

"I hate you!" she screamed. "I wish I was back with Allen. He let me do anything I wanted to!" She ran out, slamming the door behind her.

CHAPTER 7

The Day at the Shore

The next few weeks were full of ups and downs for Meg, as well as for Crow and Repulsive. There were times—when Kit was showing her how to do chores—when she was really happy. Kit was not Allen, but he did have a happy-go-lucky way that reminded Meg of her brother. Besides, she was more at home with Kit and the animals than she was with her aunt and the housework. It seemed that Aunt Laura believed there were many things she should be learning to do around the house—such as washing dishes, setting the table, making her bed, and keeping her room dusted and clean. Meg already knew how to do most of these chores. She had done them aboard the *Sea Mouse*—but only when it pleased her. Now her aunt expected her to do them every day.

Meg preferred to spend her time following Kit around and "helping" him, but Uncle Gilbert said that it was bad for the hens and disturbed them to have someone running through their pens for no purpose. He found fault, too, because Meg cracked a few eggs when she took them out of the nests and because she sometimes forgot, and packed them in the wrong cases. Meg would ask Kit many questions, and then she would find herself telling him something that her brother had once done, until her uncle would come and remind Kit that there were chores to be finished and that he was wasting time in talk.

Crow was kept in his shed after the first day, although Kit did build him a little yard, so that he could come out and take the air. He could not get into much trouble that way.

But Repulsive was able to live up to his name. As soon as he went outdoors he met the yellow cat, Timothy Two, and there was a terrible cat fight, with yellow fur—but no black fur—scattered all over the barnyard. Heather chased both cats up a maple tree, and Timothy became so terrified that he left home and would sneak back only when he thought Repulsive was in the house. On occasions, he made a mistake, and there were still more fights. Since Repulsive considered it beneath him to catch rats, they prospered during Timothy's absence.

Yet there were times when Meg was happy— when Aunt Laura said, "Your room does look much neater today, Megan," and when the new clothes came. Even if they weren't the things she had first wanted, they fitted well, were brightly colored, and had a nice new unused smell.

There was also the afternoon when Uncle Gilbert agreed that Kit might go clamming and that Meg could go along with him. They would take Heather too. Meg had already made friends with the collie, because Heather was of a loving nature and had forgiven her for that kick the first night they met. Sometimes it seemed Heather was as much her dog as Kit's, and Repulsive was very jealous of his rival.

They walked to the shore. It was not much more than a mile away, down a winding dirt road, banked with goldenrod and the last of the fall asters. Little brown rabbits scampered

across the road, and Heather dashed after them, but she was never able to find them. The shore itself was marshy; there was more mud than sand. The marsh grass had turned a rusty yellow, and little clumps of marsh rosemary still lingered in bloom.

There was no wharf or landing on this shore, nor any house to be seen. Kit showed her a little tidal brook, cut in the deep sod of the marsh. At low tide it was only a muddy trickle, while

water dropped from the raw claybanks on either side. Kit said that at high water you could float a skiff here, and that in a heavy storm the whole marsh was often flooded. Although it was not as pretty as many beaches, still it smelled of the sea, and the gulls wheeled overhead with their mournful cries.

Meg took off her sneakers and paddled around in the salty, sticky mud, while Kit hunted halfheartedly for clam holes. Meg

waded up the brook for a short distance, and
rounding a sharp corner of the banking, she
came upon a skiff, moored snugly to a big log of
driftwood. The skiff was complete with oars
and oarlocks, but it was aground in the soft
mud, and only a tiny stream of water ran under
the stern, so it was impossible to go rowing. At
high tide the skiff would be afloat.

Meg scrambled in and out of the skiff, tried
the oars in the oarlocks, and wondered if Uncle
Gilbert would let her come down here someday
at high water and go rowing. It seemed wonderful to be in a boat again—even one that was
firmly aground. At last she went to tell Kit of
her find.

"It's probably Brad Hutchins' skiff," Kit said.
"He used to keep one down here in the summertime, so as to go fishing. Maybe he hasn't taken
it up yet."

"Do you think he'd mind if I used it?" Meg
asked. "I can row awfully well."

Kit rubbed the mud off the handle of his clam
hoe. "I guess Brad wouldn't mind, but I don't
believe my dad would like it. He wouldn't let
you go out in it alone. Anyway, when school

starts, there won't be time to come down here."

"I could come on Saturdays," Meg said. "And I know all about a boat—more than your father does, anyway. Allen taught me. Why, I used to steer the *Dovekie,* and she was a real passenger boat."

"If you know so much," Kit said, "do you know where to find clams?" He had dug holes all over the flats, but he didn't have more than a dozen clams in his washer.

Meg had gone clamming many times with her brother, but she had always left the work to him and played around the shore herself. Now she began to hunt for holes, stamping her feet, as she had seen Allen do, to make the clam send up its telltale spurt of water. Kit dug some more, and then Meg took the hoe and dug. In all, they got a scant peck of clams—just enough to steam. They were covered with mud and sand, and their backs felt tired and their hands were blistered, but they believed they had done very well. The long shadows warned that the afternoon was passing.

"I've got to get back and help with the chores," Kit said.

Now that the tide was coming, Meg would have liked to stay and see the skiff afloat, but Kit would not wait. "Dad won't like it if I'm not there to pick eggs."

"Bother the old eggs!" Meg said. "How I hate hens! They always need waiting on." But she was tired herself and more content than she had been for many days. They tramped up the road, Kit carrying the washer with the clams, and Meg the clam hoe. Heather ran ahead of them. She was spattered with mud from the flats.

"We'll have to turn the hose on her when we get home," Kit said.

The road was narrow and rough and looked as if it had seldom been used by a car. Therefore, they were both startled when they heard the unmistakable purr of a motor. As they scrambled to one side, a big broad-beamed station wagon in bright blue came nosing along slowly through the tall weeds, rocking at every bump in the road. Kit whistled to Heather, and as the little collie ran to him, he caught hold of her collar and stood scowling. Meg was curious to see who would drive down such a road.

"It's Old Red," Kit whispered. Before Meg could ask who "Old Red" was, the car came to a stop beside them. She saw that there was only the driver in it and that he was getting out.

Old Red was a big man, thickset and burly-looking, without being fat. He had blond hair, so light that it was almost colorless, and pale-blue eyes. His face was broad and heavy; the fair skin had sunburned until it was red. He was smiling, an odd little twisted smile, which Meg soon saw was a part of his face and had nothing to do with his emotions.

He looked at the boy and the girl and then at the dog. "Are you keeping that cur on a leash?" he asked.

"No. Why should we?" Kit asked. It was the first time Meg had ever heard anger in his voice.

"You know what'll happen if I catch her chasing deer," the man said. "There'll be one dog less in the world."

"Heather doesn't chase deer," said Kit. "She never goes off the farm except with us."

"That's what they all say," Old Red said with a sneer. "But we've had trouble with dogs over on the preserve."

"That's no reason to pick on us," Kit said bitterly. "I wish your deer would stay at home as well as Heather does."

Old Red looked at the boy, and his eyes were like hard blue stones. "There's no need to get sassy. I'm the warden, and I have a right to check on unlicensed dogs."

"Heather's got a license," Meg said, getting into the fray. "The tag's right here on her collar."

The man stared at her now, with his little half-smile. "Whose kid are you?"

"She's my cousin," said Kit. "She's living with us."

The warden lost interest in Meg. In fact, he no longer seemed to be much concerned with the children. He lit a cigarette and got back into the car. "I'm just checking on the dogs in this neck of the woods—and the people too." He started the car and added in parting, "I'm not looking for trouble, but I can handle it if it comes."

He drove on, and Kit let the dog run free again. "I wish Heather had bit him," he said bitterly.

Meg was surprised at such resentment in her moderate-tempered cousin. "Who is he?" she asked.

"He's Old Red Carver, the game warden, and he's just as mean as he looks. He's had it in for us ever since Dad complained about the deer getting into our garden last spring. They just about ruined it."

"Why didn't you shoot them?" Meg asked.

"You can't," Kit said. "Not when it's out of season. There's a game preserve over there." He vaguely waved his hand toward the west. "Dad says the deer sneak out of it and eat our beans and then dodge back into it again."

"That warden looked really mean," Meg said. "Can he just come along and shoot any dog?"

"No, only if he catches them chasing deer."

"Well, he'd better not shoot *our* dog. She never chases anything," Meg said, not aware that this was the first time she had regarded Heather as *her* dog.

CHAPTER 8

The Runaway

Meg did not like school any better than she had thought she would. Aunt Laura was shocked when she learned how little schooling Meg had received, for although she was nearly eleven, Meg was only in the third grade.

"Allen never made me go to school," Meg said, but she saw that her aunt and uncle only put this down as one more sin that poor Allen had committed.

The teacher said kindly that very likely Meg would soon catch up with the other children—provided she studied hard. Meg had no intention of studying hard. She was ashamed to be in a class with children smaller than herself, but she didn't want to work hard enough to catch up with the others either. What she really wanted was no school at all.

Homework was one of the many things she hated. After you'd spent your day shut up in a schoolhouse, who wanted to spend the evening doing homework? Yet Aunt Laura insisted that both Meg and Kit should do their homework every night. There was no reading or playing until it was finished.

Kit took it all good-naturedly. He was not a brilliant student, but he got along well enough. Meg sulked—especially over the arithmetic, which was always her hardest subject. The long rows of numbers never added up the same way twice.

One day Meg told Aunt Laura that the teacher had not had time to hear their arithmetic lesson that day. "She told us to do the same homework as yesterday, and I've got *that* all done." To her surprise, her aunt believed the story, and Meg had a wonderfully free evening. Of course there was trouble in class the next day, when Meg didn't have her homework prepared, but she wasn't trying to please her teacher. If she could get out of doing her homework, she felt it was worth the trouble.

After this, when Meg didn't feel like preparing her arithmetic—and she didn't feel like it most of the time—she told the same fib. Of course her arithmetic got poorer and poorer, but Aunt Laura knew nothing about this.

Kit was the one who began to feel uneasy. "Meg," he said one evening, when they were alone at the kitchen table doing their lessons, "Meg, aren't you lying about your homework?"

Meg looked at her cousin with hard brown eyes. "What do you mean by 'lying'?"

"You know what I mean. I'll bet your teacher doesn't skip math every day, the way you say she does."

"How do you know what my teacher does? You aren't in my class."

"I should think you'd learn your arithmetic and get out of that class. I shouldn't think you'd want to stay with those babies."

Meg flushed. "You mind your own business, and I'll mind mine," she said cuttingly. "Or I'll make trouble for you," she added.

Kit's blue eyes were unhappy. He wasn't afraid of Meg's threat. There was little she could do in the way of making trouble for him. He knew that Meg could get into a good deal of trouble herself, but if she would not heed his warning, there was little he could do about it. He could not turn tattletale.

It was strange that Aunt Laura could have been so easily fooled. Perhaps it was because Kit had always been honest, even about his failures, and she had never encountered a child like Meg. Still, she realized there was something wrong. "Meg's teacher seems to be very lax," she told Uncle Gilbert one evening. "I wonder that she's allowed to teach at all. Meg is learning almost nothing in arithmetic. The teacher always seems to skip the lesson."

"I'd inquire into it," Uncle Gilbert said seriously. "We may have to complain to the school board if she's not teaching as she should."

So Aunt Laura wrote a letter to the teacher, asking why she neglected math so frequently. She sent the note in by way of Meg, who promptly lost it, but who did not tell this to her aunt. Meg realized now that she was getting into serious trouble, but she could not see any solution, except to go on. She lived from day to day and did not worry too much about what might happen tomorrow.

Aunt Laura was angry, because she received no answer to her note. One day she announced that tomorrow she would go in and talk with the teacher herself. It would not be easy for her to leave the farm and go into town, but there was nothing else to be done. "I don't remember that we ever had any trouble with a teacher of Kit's," Aunt Laura said. "She must be a very poor teacher."

Meg was frantic. There was no way in the world she could prevent her aunt from visiting school, and then, of course, she would learn that it was not the teacher, but Meg herself, who was at fault. So Meg decided to run away.

The idea was not a new one. It had occurred to her many times since her uncle had brought her from Summerport. It would be easy enough to give these folks the slip and return to Allen and the *Sea Mouse*. Afterward, even if her uncle called in the police to hunt for her, she was sure that Allen would be clever enough to keep away from them.

The thing that held her back was the little core of uncertainty in her heart ever since her brother's refusal to stand up to her uncle. Always there was the fear that her brother might actually have been relieved to get rid of her, that she might be unwelcome if she returned. However, now that there was nothing else for her to do, it was not too difficult for her to feel that it had not been Allen's fault after all. That old Smalley Blake was to blame.

What was it Smalley Blake had said? "He'll never know about it, kid!"

"That's what *you* think, Mr. Blake!" Meg said to herself grimly.

Just how would she get to Summerport? She was not certain of the road, and it would be a long walk. It had taken them several hours in her uncle's truck. If she tried to hitchhike a ride, she might meet someone who knew the Duncans and who would be suspicious. Anyway, she might be on the road so long that the Duncans would have plenty of time to notify the police.

Then she remembered that Kit had once told her that Summerport lay right across the bay from Heron's Neck. If there was a bridge, you could ride there in five or ten minutes, but as it was, the road wound inland in order to clear the narrow, tapering head of the bay. Meg was shrewd enough to know that the Duncans would expect her to go by the road. They were farming folks; they would never think of that skiff down there on the shore. But a boat was a thing Meg understood well.

Then she thought of her pets. How could she take them? In a heart-wrenching moment she realized that she could not. It would not be possible for her to take anything but herself. Then what would become of them? Repulsive, it was true, had endeared himself to her aunt, in spite of his battles with Timothy. Perhaps since he was a black cat—and black cats were very rare —he might be allowed to stay on the farm. But none of the Duncans could stand Crow! Since his feathers were not long enough to permit his flying away, it was horrible to think of his fate. For a few minutes she considered taking him anyway, but it would be almost impossible to get him into a bag unnoticed—he made such a racket when he was disturbed.

With a sigh, Meg hunted up a pencil and paper. Kit was her only hope. Perhaps he would be willing to look after the crow until he could take care of himself. She found the paper and printed carefully, "I am goin away. Plese take care of Crow. Meg." Then she folded the paper into a note, printed "KIT" in big letters on the outside of it, and propped it up on her dresser.

Then Meg went to her closet and laid out her warmest clothes. It would be cold on the water now that fall was here. She took out dungarees, a sweater, and a jacket.

When Aunt Laura was out of the pantry, Meg helped herself to a loaf of bread and a generous hunk of cheese. She wasn't sure just how long it would take to row to Summerport. Perhaps it would take as long as two days. Still, this should be food enough. She put the bread and

cheese in an old shoe box. Then she remembered that Allen had said that no one should
start out in a boat without drinking water. So
she filled a milk bottle with water and added
this to her collection.

Meg wrapped the shoe box and the bottle in
her sweater and hid them in an alder thicket at
the turn in the road where the school bus
stopped. She scattered handfuls of dead leaves
over them to hide them.

It was a sleepless night. Meg worried little
over the journey itself or about whether she
would have any trouble in slipping away—she
was quite confident that she could reach Summerport easily enough. But she was upset over
leaving Repulsive and Crow behind, and once
the thought entered her mind, she wondered if it
was really worth it. Wouldn't it be possible to
explain to Aunt Laura about the math? She
might be allowed to start all over again. But no,
they would have to explain it to the teacher as
well, and she would have to keep on going to
school just the same. It would be better to get
away from all these people who expected so

much from her, and get back with Allen, who
never cared what she did.

Then an uneasy thought came to her. What if
her brother was no longer in Summerport?
Where would she go then? The excursion job
had ended long ago, and Allen and the *Sea
Mouse* might well have drifted on to some other
town. But she remembered that her brother had
spoken of getting work aboard a scallop dragger
that fished out of Summerport. No doubt he was
still there. There was no point in worrying over
that until she had to. She put down, with a firm
hand, the faint but persistent thought that Allen
might not be pleased to see her, that he might
have plans in which there was no place for her.

The morning was bright and sunny, one of
those crisp October days. Meg kept her mind
fixed on Allen. As long as she could remember
that she was going back to her brother, nothing
else mattered. Allen's red head was like a beacon on which she kept her thoughts firmly cen-
tered.

In that way, she got through breakfast and
said good-by to Repulsive and Crow without

tears or sentiment. Even when Crow bowed carefully and gurgled some sounds that were like words, she was not touched. When her aunt said, "Your uncle will take me into town this afternoon," Meg merely ducked her head and said, "Yes'm."

It was lucky that Kit didn't go to the same school and thus started out early to ride to town with another boy. For this reason, there was only Meg to wait for the school bus. She quickly found the bundle that she had hidden under the leaves, and being careful to keep out of the view of the farm, she turned down the side road which led to the shore. When the bus driver found no one waiting beside the road, he would just go on to the next stop. With a little luck no one would miss her until her aunt reached school that afternoon.

The guilty feeling that she was playing hooky soon left Meg, and she began to enjoy herself. Many of the leaves had fallen. They had blown into long, rustly drifts beside the road. Sometimes Meg waded in them above her ankles.

At the smell of the sea, her heart lifted. How wonderful it smelled! And how wonderful were the sad, plaintive cries of the gulls! With the falling of the leaves, a wide expanse of road was visible, and she could see the water of the cove dancing in the sunlight. I could never live away from the sea, Meg thought.

Worries began to plague her now—that someone else might be on the shore, that the skiff might be gone, or that the tide might not yet be high enough to float it. But the shore was deserted, the tide well up, and the bubbly little ridges of foam, which worked inland over the small stones on the beach, indicated that it was still rising.

Meg ran across the strip of marshland, and there was the skiff, still lying in the tidal inlet. Meg did not see anything wrong in using the skiff without its owner's permission. After all, it was just borrowing—not stealing. She would leave the skiff at the float in Summerport, and the owner could find it easily enough.

Meg scrambled down the smooth clay banking and into the skiff. She stored her belongings under the seat and then checked the oars and oarlocks. A strong current was running up the inlet, carrying with it empty shells, bits of rockweed, and little islands of foam. The tide was against her now, but in an hour it would be slack water, and then the ebbing tide would help her.

Summerport did not lie directly across the bay. It was somewhat to the east, and the tide would carry her down onto it. But she must not let it carry her too far down, or she would find herself in the more wild and dangerous region at the entrance to the bay.

For an instant she wished she understood the lay of the land better, but she would just have to make out with what she could remember. The most important thing was to cross the bay. Then she could work along the shore to Summerport. Very likely she would remember some of the landmarks she had seen from the *Dovekie*.

She untied the skiff and slipped the oars into place, turning the bow into the current. It was good to have the quick, live feeling of a boat under her again. She pulled at the oars with all her strength. It was lucky that the skiff had been moored so near to the mouth of the inlet. In a

few minutes she was clear of the deadly, clutching current.

Meg rowed easily now, feeling out the mood and whims of the strange skiff as a rider might try out a new horse. The distant shore ran along the edge of the bright horizon like a long black finger. For a moment Meg wavered. The bay looked very wide, the finger of land very distant. She thought of following along the shore line, but that would double the journey and be no better than walking. Then she put down the faint uneasiness. After all, she had rowed ever since she had lived aboard the *Sea Mouse*. She knew just as much about a skiff as Allen did, she was sure, and her brother would think nothing of rowing across the bay. So she turned the skiff's bow toward the black finger of the mainland and started rowing.

CHAPTER 9

The Return

Meg had rowed a good deal during the summer, but it had been two months now since she had been in a boat, and she had grown soft. Furthermore, the bay was at least five miles wide at this point, and that would be a good row for a man —to say nothing of a ten-year-old.

The day was mild and sunny, without wind —one of those fall days that seem to be left over from summer. There was not a ripple on the water, or the sight of anything but a shag, beating its way south. It looked like a duck, except for its long, scrawny neck. I wish I could fly, Meg thought. I'd be there by now.

The little cove and the shore that led back to the farm had grown fainter behind her, but the other shore did not seem any nearer. The

128

tide had turned, Meg guessed, for she noticed that a large square-topped hill, which had been directly in front of her, had now slipped to the north. She was dropping down the bay, in spite of her effort to keep in a straight line. She inspected her hands. They were sore and blistered, and her arms ached too. The skiff rowed twice as hard as it had an hour ago.

She decided that she was hungry, so she pulled in the oars and got out the shoe box from under the seat. Of course the skiff would drift with the tide, but it wouldn't hurt if she did drift down on Summerport. Meg ate the bread and cheese. She thought of her Aunt Laura, arriving at school and finding her absent. For the first time, the wish came to her that she *had* done her math the way she should have. Then none of this would have ever come about. Then she thought of Allen, and her courage returned.

When she had eaten some bread and cheese and taken a mouthful of water from her bottle, she turned her attention back to rowing. There was no use in deceiving herself; she was not making the progress she had intended to make. She must reach Summerport by dark, for there was no place to stop, and she could not row by night. But the sun had started down into the west, and she was not halfway across.

Rowing seemed harder now, for her hands were sore, and her arms ached. "I wish I'd never started," Meg said. "Leastways, I wish I'd walked." Walking wouldn't have been any harder or taken any longer.

The sun began to drop down toward the dark blue hills that lay beyond Summerport. Meg's hand was terribly sore. She looked at it and found that the blister on the palm had broken. If only there was a boat of some sort around—

they might give her a tow. But the bay seemed deserted, and now the shore behind her was as far away as the one in front of her.

With the approach of evening, the air had turned chilly. Even rowing could not keep her warm, and she was glad that she had thought to bring a sweater. Meg was forced, too, to face a fact that she had ignored as long as possible— that she wasn't going to reach Summerport that day. The frightening thought came into her mind that she might not reach it at all. She had no anchor, and anyway, the water was probably far too deep for a small anchor. There was no way for her to tell the right direction in the dark, and if the skiff drifted with the tide all night, it was impossible to tell where it might land.

Meg had only a hazy memory of the bay south of Summerport. What little she had seen from the *Dovekie* she had soon forgotten. She thought that there were several islands, and perhaps she could land on one of them. Otherwise, she might drift past them in the dark and go out to sea. Meg saw now how foolish she had been to attempt this journey. A stiff breeze would almost certainly swamp the skiff. She had thought that she knew everything about the sea—just because she could row around the harbor—but she was so far away from shore now that to return was impossible.

The sun dropped down behind the hills back of Summerport. The fall twilight was brief, and although the day had been sunny, the night was chilly. Even with a sweater on, Meg felt the cold.

She ate some more of the bread and cheese and wondered what her aunt had done when she reached the school. Perhaps she had called the police, and they might be looking for her by now. It occurred to her that Kit might have remembered the skiff, and the thought brought almost a sense of relief. But it was growing dark, and there was no other boat anywhere in sight.

For the first time she fully realized that she could not row all night. She would have no idea of what direction she was heading. Tired, sleepy, and cold as she was, she was filled with despair. Suddenly a light appeared before her, winking like a star. Some house, located on the heavily wooded shore north of Summerport, had an outdoor light, which sparkled as bravely as any lighthouse.

Meg felt her courage return with the light. It was like a beacon on the lonely shore and gave her a sense of direction. But her courage did not last long. Her hands were blistered, her arms ached, and she rowed so slowly that the tide, which had turned and was running inland, carried her slowly above the light.

Meg tried to fix her mind on Allen, Summerport, and the *Sea Mouse,* but they all seemed oddly far away. Even the memory of Allen faded, until he was more like someone she had known a long, long time ago. The strange thing was that what she could remember the best was the kitchen at the Duncan farm, brightly lighted and warm, with her aunt and uncle and Kit, all sitting around the table, while Heather hopefully pushed her nose under the tablecloth begging for food.

Meg pulled in the oars. She was stiff with cold and from sitting still for so long, and she was so sleepy she could no longer keep her eyes open. The light on the shore had vanished.

She crawled off the seat and down into the bottom of the boat, where the cold did not reach. She wondered dully why she had ever been foolish enough to start on this adventure. Her troubles at school no longer seemed important.

Suddenly Meg awoke. A sharp jar ran through the skiff, followed by a harsh, grating sound. The smooth rocking motion of a boat in the water changed to the dull grinding of a boat aground.

Meg rubbed her eyes. She was still stiff and cold, and her feet had gone to sleep. A wave, striking the side of the skiff, poured cold water down her neck and brought her to life. It was pitch-dark, and while she knew that the skiff was aground on something, she couldn't tell if it was a ledge or a beach.

The sea was alive with phosphorescence. Wherever the waves touched the skiff it was bathed in cold fire. From the line of pale-green flame, Meg guessed that she had come ashore on some beach, and not merely a submerged rock. There were no waves, just little ripples of water, followed by the rattling suck of the undertow. The skiff had come in side-on, grounded a moment, pulled away, and then grounded again.

Meg scrambled over the side, feeling the ice-cold water soak through her sneakers. She got hold of the bow of the skiff and, on the next ripple, gave a good hard pull. She was not strong enough to get the skiff more than a few inches up on the beach, but she knew very well that she must not let it float away. Her hand touched the metal ring in the bow. There was a rope looped through the ring. If I can only find a big rock, Meg thought, as she groped about in the dark. Then she stumbled over a log of driftwood, lodged in the fine sand. There was a stub of a branch that made a good place to tie the rope.

She crawled back to the skiff once more, for in the darkness it was impossible to see where she had landed. The dew had fallen, and the seats of the skiff were clammy and cold. Meg felt very tired, but she was restless, too, and her throat hurt when she swallowed. Her feet were wet and icy, but her face seemed to be on fire, and her head pounded.

Meg curled up like a puppy on the hard, damp boards that formed the bottom of the skiff. If only she were back in her bedroom at the farm!

In spite of the cold and the uncomfortable bed, she must have fallen asleep again, for when she woke up, the sky above her head was bright with the morning. Meg sat up and sniffled. It was more than a sniffle of sorrow. There was no doubt about it—she had caught cold. There was

the stuffed-up nose, the sore throat—all the horrible, wretched feeling that went with a cold.

Before, whenever she had a cold, she had
been able to lie snugly in her bunk, while Allen
brought her ice cream for her poor raw throat.
Now she must get out and shift for herself. She
couldn't lie forever in a skiff tied to a log.

Meg sat up and looked around. The long
sandy beach curved before her without a sign of
a house. Nothing looked familiar. She couldn't
even tell if she was on an island or if she had
reached the other side of the bay.

"I suppose I'll have to walk until I come to some house," she said to herself. She worried briefly about the skiff. It was "borrowed," and so nothing must happen to it. But it was aground now, and there seemed to be nothing she could do about it. She made sure that the knot was tight before she started on her way.

She stopped suddenly. Surely that was the sound of a motor that she heard! A small boat nosed out around the point of land to the north. The rising sun glinted on its cabin windows as it heaved to. It was a lobster man, out early in the morning tending his traps.

Meg began to wave her arms frantically—her throat was too sore for shouting. The lobster man gave no sign that he had noticed her. After all, the boat was quite a way offshore.

Meg ran back to the skiff and found the jacket, which she had discarded, because it was wet. Now she waved it wildly in the air, and she was encouraged to see the little figure in the stern of the boat hesitate after he had pushed the trap overboard. Then he began to nose the boat slowly inshore.

Meg watched him. She could not row out to the boat, for she would never be able to get the

skiff afloat until the tide rose. When the lobster man had come in as close as he dared, he anchored and made ready to come ashore in his own skiff.

He was a little old man in heavy rubber boots and yellow oilskins, but to Meg, he looked like an angel. She felt like throwing her arms around his neck, but instead, she sat down on the edge of her skiff and wiped her nose.

"What's wrong, kid?" the lobster man asked.

"I'm lost." Meg's voice came out in a squeak. "I rowed away from home, and I got lost."

"Well," the man said, trying to comfort her, "now you're found. Where did you say your home was?"

"Over to the Duncan farm at Heron's Neck," Meg said. "I want to go back there."

It was not until she was in the cockpit of the lobster boat, wrapped in an old blanket that smelled of fish and gasoline, that the thought came to her—but I was going to Summerport! By then it didn't seem worth the trouble to try and explain it to the old fisherman, and in her heart she wasn't sorry to be going back to the farm.

Meg sat in the cockpit and sniffled and coughed. For once, she felt no interest in a boat. She described to the old man the marsh, the mud flats, and the little tidal brook, until he understood where she had come from. "But that's five miles away, child!" he said. "You must have drifted with the tide."

Meg didn't tell him that she had run away. She could see that he thought she had been out rowing and that the tide had carried her off-shore. He kept muttering about parents who allowed their children out alone in a boat.

A truck was parked where the wood road ended on the beach, and several people were walking along the shore. Meg felt very sick, and she was almost happy over it, for if she *was* sick, there would be no possibility of a scolding. But scolding or not, it was a relief when they all crowded around her—Uncle Gilbert, Kit, and Aunt Laura, who was wiping the tears away on a corner of her apron.

"Found her on Butter Island—five miles from here," the old lobster man said. "You'd better get her to bed. She's caught cold or something. Don't know why anyone would let a little kid out in a boat alone. It's a wonder she was ever found!"

"Oh, you poor sick lamb," Aunt Laura cried. "I've been frantic, Megan! I was afraid you were drowned!" Meg felt herself lifted up and enfolded in a warm blanket of love.

CHAPTER 10

The *Pumpkin Seed*

Meg was sick in bed for several weeks. It was almost November before she could start school once more. Neither Uncle Gilbert nor Aunt Laura ever scolded her for running away. Instead, they seemed silent and a little uneasy, for they had been badly frightened by her behavior. Aunt Laura said that the teacher would permit her to make up the homework in math. "And I will help you with your lessons," she added. But nothing more was said.

Kit was in and out of her room every day, bringing all the news and the gossip of the farm. "Pulsive was run over by a car the day you went," Kit said. "But he hasn't used up all of his nine lives, 'cause he went right under the car on one side and came out on the other and wasn't

144

hurt a bit. Only it's made him very nervous. He thinks all cars are after him."

Repulsive stretched himself across Meg's ribs and worked his claws into the blanket. He sang loudly and stared at her with moon-yellow eyes. Ever since Meg had come back she was allowed to have the cat on the bed. It made Heather very jealous, and she would push her head under Meg's arm to call attention to herself.

Once in a while Kit even brought Crow in to visit, and Aunt Laura said nothing, even though Crow was a great pest. He loved to be in the house, where there were so many interesting things to destroy. He would walk around rapidly, looking carefully at every new object, upsetting cups, stealing bobby pins, and tearing curtains. But then there came a day when Crow bowed carefully, spread out his wings, and made a queer gurgling noise in his throat.

"Go on," Kit urged. "Say it."

"Hello! Hello!" Crow almost shouted it, and Kit beamed with pride.

"Oh, Kit," Meg said. "He can talk! He's really a talking crow! Did you teach him?"

"Well," Kit admitted, "I did keep saying

'Hello' over and over. But I think he would have caught on anyway. He's a very bright crow."

One day Meg said, "Kit, when I'm well enough to go back to school, do you suppose some Saturday we could go down to the shore clamming again?"

Kit looked at her rather queerly. "Do you really want to go down to the shore? I shouldn't think you'd want to see the water again after you almost drowned."

"I didn't almost drown," Meg said indignantly. "I was all right, and I rowed well, only I got tired. It was too long a row. I wish Uncle Gilbert had a skiff," she added.

"Well, he won't ever have one," Kit said.

"Why not? It's not very far to the shore. We could have fun if you had a skiff."

"Dad had a brother who was drowned," Kit answered slowly. "I don't know much about it. Dad never speaks of it. But I know he hates the water, and he never would own a boat of any kind."

"You mean we had an uncle who was drowned?" Meg asked in sudden interest. Then the thought came to her, "Maybe that's why he doesn't like the Elwells either, because they had boats and were around the water."

It appeared that the running away had done some good after all. Meg seemed to have got some of the meanness out of her system. Or perhaps she had become resigned to living on a farm. For a long time she had hoped that she might get a letter from her brother—at least a picture post card—but finally she even gave up looking for that. Meg did much better in her schoolwork and even started to master arithmetic. She also learned to help Kit with the hens, gathering and packing eggs without breaking a single one.

Her birthday came early in November, and it was Kit who thought of the present for her, although he had a hard time convincing his father. "I know what Meg wants, more than anything," he said one day. "That's a skiff of her own. And I know a fellow who's got one for sale—a little one, just Meg's size."

"Not a boat!" his father said in alarm. "Why, she's just got to the point where she's stopped talking about the water."

"She thinks about it just the same," said Kit. "The other day she asked me if I thought she could earn enough money weeding gardens this summer to buy that old skiff of Brad's."

His father shook his head. "I'd rather she forgot about boats and the water."

But in the end he weakened enough to go and look at the skiff, and it did seem to be just Megan's size. The owner assured him that it was quite safe—even for a little girl—and that some calking and paint would make it quite seaworthy.

"Megan cannot be allowed to use it alone," he told Kit, after he had bought the skiff. "Some older person must be with her whenever she takes it out."

"But Dad," Kit objected, "she's rowed all over the bay now, and she knows more about a boat than any of us."

It was cold on her birthday. The first snow was falling. Uncle Gilbert and Kit led her out to the barn, and there on the floor of the darkened grain room sat a small flat-bottomed skiff. It was snowy white on the outside, and on the

inside it was painted the brightest of blues. The tiny railing that ran around its edge was jet-black.

Meg caught her breath. "Is it mine?"

It was lovelier than any skiff she could remember seeing at Summerport. She ran her hands tenderly over the newly painted sides, over the little curved seat that just fitted into the bow, and over the brand-new oarlocks that could be lifted out and folded back.

Her uncle cleared his throat. "It was really Kit's idea, but we all thought that—well, that it might make you happier here with us."

Meg turned to him with shining eyes. "Oh, Uncle Gil! Even Allen never gave me a skiff of my own, though of course his skiff was mine, too, in a way. We both shared it," she added loyally.

She saw a look of pain in her uncle's eyes, and for the first time she wished she hadn't mentioned Allen's name. "What shall I name it?" she asked quickly, to cover up her blunder.

"That's easy," said Kit. "I can think of dozens of names. How about *Pumpkin Seed?* It's just about as small as one."

Meg shook her head. "I think I'll call her—" And then she stopped. She was going to say, "*Sea Mouse the Second,*" but she remembered just in time. After a moment she said, "All right, Kit. It was your idea. We'll call her the *Pumpkin Seed.*"

"Of course you can't put it into the water until spring," said Uncle Gilbert. "And remember, Megan, you are never to go out in it alone. Next summer you must take swimming lessons, and we'll find someone to teach you how to handle a boat properly."

Meg was on the point of saying, "But I *know*

how to handle it properly," but she held her tongue. She saw that her uncle had made a great concession when he overcame his dislike of the water enough to allow her to have the skiff. It was only fair that she should abide by his rules.

CHAPTER 11

Allen Returns

It was a rainy May morning—the gentle rain of spring. A wet Saturday usually meant late rising, but Megan was up already, her nose pressed against the windowpane.

"Surely you're not going down to the shore this morning," Aunt Laura said. "Even if it stops raining, everything will be damp."

"But I've got to go," said Meg, "and see if there's any water in the skiff. I can wear my raincoat. And I want to take something to eat, because I may not be back to lunch."

Kit came in, shaking the water from his oilskins. "It's stopped raining. It's just misty now."

"I don't know why you want to tramp to the shore on a day like this," her aunt fretted.

"Oh, let her go," Kit said. "She wants to bail the skiff and make sure it's all right."

Meg put on her new jacket and her rubber boots. Then she put some sandwiches and cookies into the tin lunch pail that she carried to school, and made some hot cocoa for the Thermos. "Can I take Heather?" she asked.

"Good idea," Kit said. "She needs the run."

"I wish you were coming too. We could have a real picnic."

"Not a chance. Dad wants me to help him move some hens."

"You know, I think I'll take the hoe and see if I can get some clams."

She was on her way to the tool shed to find the hoe when she saw Crow. He was standing by a corner of the porch, pulling off tulip blossoms, and tearing them to bits.

"Oh, Crow!" Meg cried. "Can't you be near anything without destroying it?"

Crow spread out his wings and bowed carefully. "Hello!" he shouted. "Hello! Hello!" But his eyes were bright and evil.

Meg stopped and rubbed his head, which he adored, but while his eyes were blissfully closed, she seized him. There was a yell of fury from Crow and a yell of pain from Meg as he bit her. It was impossible to avoid Crow's huge beak. Meg held onto him just the same and ran as fast as she could to the old chicken yard, which served as his prison.

She dumped him in as quickly as she could. Just as she thought, she had forgotten to brace a stick against the door, and Crow had jerked on it until it had come unhooked. His yard was large, but he was always getting out of it, and once he was out, he would tear up everything he could find. Sometimes he would pick the flowers and carry them to the front door and then shout "Hello!" until someone opened the door. Then he would drop the flowers and bow, as if to say, "See what I've ruined!"

Meg soon found the clam hoe, and putting her dinner bucket into an empty pail, she started off with Heather running in circles around her. The rain had stopped, but water still dripped softly from the trees. Robins sang, their voices full and sweet in the dampness. The wild plum and the wild pear trees were in blossom, and the wind had shaken their petals over the road like snow.

The shore was gray and lonely, deserted even

by the gulls. A heavy mist still hung over the water. A kingfisher, disturbed at his fishing in the tidal brook, rattled noisily and flew away. Heather raced in pursuit and then gave it up.

The *Pumpkin Seed* lay snugly under the high bank of the brook, the only boat on the whole shore that early in the season. It was really too cold to have the skiff in the water, because the weather was often bad in the early spring, but Meg had not been able to wait. Even if she couldn't use the *Pumpkin Seed* until her uncle was convinced that she knew how to handle a skiff, still it was some satisfaction to have the boat on the shore and to be able to come down and look after her.

With a sense of pride, Meg saw that there was only a little water in the skiff, the result of the night's rain. The *Pumpkin Seed* did not leak any more. Meg found the old coffee can that served as a bailing dish and carefully bailed out the rain water. If she learned to swim this summer perhaps her uncle would let her take the skiff out alone.

It was cold on the beach, and the tide had not ebbed enough for clamming. Meg's fingers ached. Even if it was spring, the water was chilly. Heather had found a squirrel's hide-out under the roots of an old tree and was busy digging and sniffing. Meg tucked the coffee can back under the skiff's seat and blew on her cold fingers. Then she picked up the pail and clam hoe and looked for a good place to eat her lunch.

A big maple tree grew on the edge of the beach, not far from the mouth of the brook. There was a high bank of fine sand at its foot. A log of driftwood, pressed into the sand by a winter gale, was fairly dry, and the spot was sheltered from the wind. Meg sat down on the log and opened her lunch pail.

The sea smelled so strong and so good that Meg took deep whiffs of it. Heather, quick to spot the lunch pail, left the squirrel hole and came to sit by her knee. The sad brown eyes watched her mistress's every move. Meg unwrapped the lunch carefully. There wasn't much of it—just a pleasant in-between-meal snack.

A growl rumbled in Heather's throat, and the fur stood up on her ruff. Meg looked up quickly. Two men were walking along the edge of the

shore. The fog made it impossible to see them clearly, but they appeared to be walking arm in arm.

Meg was surprised but not afraid. It was not the kind of weather in which people go walking along the shore just for the fun of it, but they might be clam diggers, waiting for the tide to ebb. She tried to hush the dog, but Heather, convinced that the strangers were dangerous, rushed toward them, barking.

The men stopped abruptly, almost in alarm. Clearly they had not noticed the child and the dog, out of sight as they were on the other side of the tree. With a sigh, Meg closed the lunch pail and went to call off the dog.

"Come here, Heather!" she called. "Heather, will you come here!"

One of the men spoke harshly. "Meg!"

Meg whirled around at the voice. The man was young and roughly dressed in an old brown jacket and rubber boots, but the hair that showed under the rim of his cap was dark-red.

"Allen!" Meg cried. "Allen!" And heedless of the dog's yelps, she ran to her brother. She threw her arms around his chest, which was as

high as she could reach, and hugged him.

"Easy now, kid," Allen said. "You'll make me drop old Smalley." But he gave in and hugged her too, while she burrowed her face in the old jacket, which smelled of salt and gasoline. "My little old Megan," Allen said.

"Is there anyone else hanging around?" Smalley Blake asked.

Meg withdrew her nose from Allen's jacket and looked at Smalley Blake with a cold eye. "What's wrong with *him*?" she asked.

"He hurt his foot," Allen answered. "Slipped

on some rockweed and turned his ankle. *Is* there anyone around, Meg?"

"No," Meg said, too happy to notice anything odd about the question. "Heather—that's the dog—and I just came down to the shore for a picnic."

"Heck of a day for a picnic," Smalley Blake said. Then he added, "You mean you got food around?"

"Do you want a sandwich, Allen?" Meg asked. She guided them toward the old log. "How did you ever get here, and where's the *Sea Mouse?*"

Allen was silent as he helped his companion. Meg saw that there was something wrong with Smalley Blake's left foot. The rubber boot had been slashed open to relieve the swelling, and he leaned heavily on Allen's shoulder. Her brother looked tired too, and Meg wondered how far they had walked.

"Where's the *Mouse?*" she asked again.

Allen eased his companion down on the log. "Sorry, Meg, but I'm afraid you won't see the old *Mouse* again."

"Why?" Meg asked. "You haven't sold her?"

"He sold her all right," Smalley Blake said, with a harsh laugh.

Allen ignored him. "We had a streak of bad luck, Meg," he said. "Ran her on the rocks—literally. We were in a hurry, and I wasn't as careful as I should have been."

"Oh, Allen!" said Meg, almost in tears. "The poor old *Mouse!* Can't something be done for her?"

" 'Fraid not," Allen said. "Where's that picnic you were talking about?"

Meg got the dinner pail. "I haven't touched anything."

"I swear, but we're lucky, Smalley!" her brother said. "What's in the Thermos? Coffee? No, cocoa. Well, it's hot anyway."

Smalley Blake scowled. "What I'd like to know is, how are we going to get out of this mess?"

Allen gave one sandwich to Smalley and bit into the other with real pleasure. "Do you want some?" he asked Meg.

She shook her head. "Allen, what's wrong?"

"Nothing to worry you," her brother answered.

Smalley Blake eased his bad leg out onto the soft sand. "Just a streak of bad luck, made worse by your dumb brother."

"I'm not going to have a shooting to top everything else. The whole plan was bad. Now the boat's gone, and we're in a jam."

"She was nothing but a rotten tub, and she'd be too hot now. Every warden would have an eye out for her. I only wish I hadn't twisted this cursed foot."

Allen took a swallow of cocoa and said nothing.

"Why is the warden looking for you?" Meg asked. "What's happened?"

Allen didn't answer, but Smalley Blake said, "Your brother's been jacking a few whitetails on the game preserve, and the warden caught up with us. We've been playing hide-and-seek ever since."

Meg thought for a moment. "What's 'jacking'?" she asked.

"Hunting, against the law," Allen said briefly.

Meg remembered the warden with the flat red face and the threatening words. "Is Old Red Carver one of them?"

"How did you know?"

"He stopped us once—Kit and me—and asked about Heather—if she was chasing deer. He was mean about it."

"If we could get to the other side of the bay, we'd be all right. They never did get a good look at us."

From their talk, Meg gathered that after she had left Summerport, Allen had taken up with Smalley Blake and the "job" he promised. They had hunted deer illegally all winter, selling the meat to a dealer. Allen was sick of the job, which paid little and was highly dangerous, and by spring he had decided to quit. But by then the game wardens were on their trail. They had abandoned the *Sea Mouse* after she went aground, and the skiff, in which they came ashore, strained a plank and leaked too badly to be of any use. Unluckily, Smalley Blake had injured his ankle at the same time, and their chance of holing up somewhere along the shore until dark, and then walking out, looked pretty gloomy.

"Come home with me, Allen," Meg said. "We've got a big barn, and the back end of it is hardly used, except to store grain and shavings. You could hide there and then walk to town tonight."

"Smalley could never make it," Allen said.

"Why don't you leave him?" Meg asked.

Allen flushed, and Smalley Blake said with a laugh, "Your sister's a credit to you, Allen."

"You don't leave your friends when they get into trouble," Allen pointed out.

"But he's not your friend," said Meg.

"Why?"

"Last fall he was the one who told Uncle Gilbert where to find me. I heard my uncle thank him."

There was a dead silence. Allen stared at Smalley Blake, his face turning as red as his hair.

Smalley Blake cleared his throat nervously. "The kid misunderstood me, Allen. Everything was at sixes and sevens that day. The old man just thanked me for giving him a hand with the luggage."

"You said Allen would never know," Meg answered bitterly. "When I said I'd tell him, you said I'd never get the chance."

"You dirty skunk," said Allen in a low voice. "If you could stand up on your own feet, I'd beat the head off you. Did this blasted poaching job mean so much to you that you squealed on us? You know the kid was the only thing I ever cared for."

Smalley Blake said nothing, and Allen continued. "I've a good mind to let you get out of this mess yourself. I never should have got mixed up in it."

"It would serve him right," Meg said. "Are you coming with me, Allen?"

But Smalley Blake, still crunching on his sandwich, had the last word. "He can't do it, kid. He can't afford to have the wardens pick me up and find out who's been working with me this winter. Like I said, no one knows us now, but if they pick me up, they're going to know about your brother quick enough."

"You never were much good, Smalley," Allen said, as if talking to himself. "I'd have known it long ago, if I'd listened to my own common sense. But after the kid was gone, it didn't seem to be worth listening. But you're right about one thing. This isn't the time or place to quit."

Smalley Blake reached for the Thermos of cocoa. "You mean you're going on with me?"

"Yes."

"You're not a bad guy, Allen—even if you are somewhat of a fool." He went on more kindly. "I didn't mean to hurt the kid. You know yourself that you weren't taking the right care of her, and she certainly doesn't look abused now."

Allen turned to his sister. "You getting along all right?"

"Oh yes," Meg said, her troubles forgotten. "Uncle Gil isn't bad, and neither is Aunt Laura. And I really like Kit—he's my cousin. Of course I have to go to school. I had some trouble at first, but things aren't so bad now. And they let me keep Pulsive and Crow. You should see Crow, Allen! He can talk now. Then there's Heather— that's the dog. And on my birthday Uncle Gil and Aunt Laura gave me a skiff of my own."

Smalley Blake pricked up his ears. "A skiff? Where is it?"

"No," said Allen. "You're not getting Meg into this mess."

"Would my skiff help you, Allen?" Meg asked in uncertainty.

Smalley Blake answered before Allen could. "It would mean we could get across the bay without being caught. We'll never make it on foot, not with this leg of mine."

"We're not taking the kid's skiff," Allen said again.

"It's right in the brook there, Allen," Meg said eagerly. "Oars are in it and everything. They'll think it went adrift."

Smalley Blake pushed away the dinner pail and got heavily to his feet. "You'll stand there till the fog lifts, Allen, and the blasted warden shows up."

"I hate to do this, Meg," her brother said, wavering. "But we're sunk if we don't find another boat."

"I know," Meg said. "I want you to have it."

Allen had little trouble getting the skiff into the water, while Smalley Blake waited on the shore.

"It's a nice boat, isn't it?" Meg said wistfully. "Uncle Gil bought it specially for my birthday."

"It is a fine boat," Allen agreed, his mind on other things. He helped Smalley Blake into the skiff. Then he drew her against him for an instant. "Thank you, Meg."

She sniffed back the tears. There was no time for such things. "Good-by, Allen. Good luck."

They pushed off quickly to make the best possible use of the fog. Allen lifted his hand once in farewell. Then the skiff was swallowed up in the mist.

CHAPTER 12

The Missing Skiff

The fog closed in, blotting out every familiar field and tree. The drip of the moisture from the trees was a melancholy sound. Meg knew that the fog was a blessing to Allen, but her own sorrow and uneasiness were intensified by it.

Heather seemed to sense her mistress's mood. It was a woebegone pair that dragged into the dooryard, Meg stumping along in rubber boots that were too big for her, the collie, head and tail down, walking behind her.

"How's the *Pumpkin Seed?*" Kit asked.

"All right," Meg said briefly, but she hung around the grain-room door, seeking comfort from his presence.

"Get any clams?"

"I didn't try," said Meg. She realized that Kit

was looking at her curiously. Shivering a little, she said, "The fog makes me think of death!"

"You must be catching cold," Kit said unromantically. "You'd better go into the house and have Mother give you something hot to drink."

"I'm all right," Meg said. She would have liked to ask Kit what happened if the wardens caught anyone killing deer out of season, but she could think of no excuse for such an odd question, so at last she went into the house.

The Duncans always got up early in the morning. Sunday was the one day they could sleep late, so when a car began blowing its horn in their dooryard at half-past five the next morning, it caused great confusion. Heather began to bark wildly. Crow, as good as any watchdog, cawed at the top of his lungs. Repulsive hid under the barn, and Uncle Gilbert muttered to himself as he went downstairs.

Neither Kit nor Aunt Laura bothered to get up, but Meg was awake at the first blast of the horn. She tumbled out of bed, her teeth chattering with cold. In the yard below there was a blue station wagon. Now her teeth chattered with something more than cold, and her heart began to pound. There was no mistaking the big light-haired man at the wheel.

Meg's thought was that Allen and Smalley Blake had been caught and that Old Red Carver had come to arrest her for helping them. She didn't care. If Allen went to jail, then she would go with him. She dressed as quickly as she could and ran downstairs.

Uncle Gilbert had hushed the dog and was at the door talking with the warden. "No, we haven't seen any strangers around here. Whom would we see at this hour of the morning?"

"I'm looking for a couple of fellows who have been shooting deer. Found their skiff up the shore a ways, with a plank stove in. Figure I must be hot on their trail. Most likely they're holed up around here somewhere."

Uncle Gilbert shook his head. "I'm sorry. I haven't seen anyone."

"It could be they were around without your seeing them," Old Red Carver said. "You've never been too co-operative about this business —always complaining about the deer getting into your garden."

"I've always upheld the law." Uncle Gilbert's voice was harsh.

"All the same, I wouldn't be surprised if you winked at those who didn't. I guess I'll have a look around your buildings."

"Do you have a search warrant?" Uncle Gilbert asked bluntly.

Old Red hesitated. He did not have such a warrant, and he could see that Gilbert Duncan was not an easy man to bluff. "I could get one fast enough," he said.

"Then you had better do it before you try searching this place."

"I may do just that," Old Red said. "You're acting mighty odd about the whole business." He got into the car and drove away.

Uncle Gilbert watched him silently. It was not until he turned around that he was aware of his audience. "Why, Megan," he said in astonishment, "did he wake you up?" Then seeing how frightened she looked, he added, "There's nothing to worry about. Red's mostly bluster, but I suppose he is trying to do his job. If he hadn't riled me up, I'd have let him look around without a warrant."

"Will he catch them?" Meg asked miserably.

"In time, I expect." Her uncle shrugged. "Red is no fool in spite of his bluster, and the wardens have a good force. But there's no need for you to be frightened. I know there's no one hiding around here."

"But—" Meg said, and then she stopped. She wanted to tell her uncle about Allen and the *Pumpkin Seed,* and she wanted to ask his advice. But she didn't dare to. She didn't know what he would do.

"Red said they had stove in a plank on their skiff." Uncle Gilbert stopped abruptly. "I'll be doggoned if I didn't forget that skiff of yours down on the shore. Was it all right when you were down there yesterday, Megan?"

"Yes," Meg managed to say, but she looked anything but happy.

Her uncle glanced at her sharply. "What's wrong, child?" he asked. Then he said, not unkindly, "You've looked upset ever since you came home yesterday."

Meg did not answer.

Her uncle went on. "You say the skiff was all right when you were down there. You didn't use it yesterday, did you? You know that you promised not to use it when you were alone."

"I haven't used it," Meg said, but even to her own ears, her answer sounded weak.

"After we've had breakfast we'll go down and check on the skiff. I doubt if there's anything wrong down there, but I wish I'd remembered to mention it when Carver was here. He'll think I had something to hide."

Breakfast was a gloomy meal. Uncle Gilbert was still angry over his brush with Old Red Carver, and Aunt Laura was upset when she learned that there might be strangers prowling about. "And criminals at that!"

Meg merely picked at her food, tormented by two questions. What would her uncle say when he found the *Pumpkin Seed* was gone? And had Allen reached a place of safety? Only Kit, undisturbed by it all, ate a good meal.

"We're going down to check on Megan's skiff," Uncle Gilbert said after breakfast. "We'll be back in time for church."

"Am I to go too?" Meg whispered to her cousin.

"Of course," Kit said in surprise. "Aren't you interested in your own boat?"

The fog was rapidly blowing away. Only patches of mist still remained over the lowland. Robins ran along the road in front of their truck.

"Someone's been here before us," Kit said. There were fresh tire tracks in the damp earth of the wood road. When they rounded the last clump of spruces and the shore came into view, they could see the blue station wagon parked there. "Oh-oh!" Kit said. "Now we're in for trouble!"

Old Red Carver was already climbing up the sloping beach, his face dark-red and his eyes hard and angry. "Why didn't you tell me you had a skiff down here?" he roared.

For once Gilbert Duncan spoke mildly, for he felt that he was in the wrong. "To tell the truth, I forgot about it until after you had gone. It belongs to Megan here, and it's been used only once since it was put in the water, so it slipped my mind at the time."

"I'll bet it did! You thought I wouldn't find out about it."

"I intended to tell you about it as soon as I made sure it was safe."

Old Red Carver gave a loud snort that might have passed for a laugh—only there was no laughter in his face. "It's safe enough all right. You let those blasted poachers have it."

"Then it's gone," Uncle Gilbert said, but his voice showed no surprise. He had been afraid of this all along. Not that the poachers had stolen it—he was doubtful if they had ever been near it—but that Megan had used the skiff the day before and failed to tie it properly.

He had felt from the beginning that Megan knew something unpleasant about the skiff. It could not have had anything to do with the poachers. She would have surely mentioned it if she had seen strangers around her skiff, so it could only be that she had disobeyed his ruling and used the skiff. Then she had lied to him, and it was clear that she had felt guilty about the whole affair. In her hurry to leave the skiff as she had found it, she must have failed to tie it securely, and it had gone adrift. No doubt it would be picked up by some lobster man, but it was unlucky that it had to happen at a time when Red Carver was already up in arms over this poaching business. The most serious part of it was that it seemed that Megan, after having been on good behavior for several months, had proved to be untrustworthy again.

He became aware that Red Carver was still talking. "You've got yourself into hot water at last. I'm going to report this to the sheriff. I wouldn't be surprised if you let them have the boat yourself."

"I can assure you that the skiff hasn't been lent to anyone!" Gilbert Duncan said coldly. "It's my belief that the boat was poorly tied and went adrift by itself." He looked at Meg, who hung her head.

"It looks suspicious to me," Carver went on. "You knew I was looking for those guys and that they had wrecked their boat. Yet you forgot to mention you had a skiff on the shore. I never would have known anything about it if I hadn't been talking to Jed Perkins and he spoke of it."

"It's still true that I didn't remember about the skiff until after you had gone. I intended to report it as soon as we had checked on it."

"Well, you'll have a chance to tell the judge

about it," Red Carver said. "You'll probably have to appear in court Monday."

Gilbert Duncan ignored the warden and turned to Meg and Kit. "Come on, children. We promised to be back in time for church."

"Do you really think those men took the skiff?" Kit asked, when they were in the truck.

"I don't believe it," his father said. "I still think it went adrift. Are you sure you didn't use it, Megan?"

"Yes," Meg said, but it wasn't a very definite yes.

CHAPTER 13

The Farewell

Heather was the first one out of the truck when they drove into the farmyard. She began barking at once, and a stranger stepped out from the shadow of the grain-house door. Meg gave a sharp cry. It was Allen.

Gilbert Duncan frowned. He recognized young Elwell at once, but of course he did not know that Allen was one of the poachers. He thought that Megan's brother must have come there to look for a handout.

Meg raced to her brother, and Allen caught her in his arms and lifted her off her feet. "Oh, Allen!" she whispered in his ear. "What are you doing here? Old Red Carver's out looking for you!"

"And I'm looking for him!"

Uncle Gilbert came up. "What can I do for you, Elwell?" he asked grimly.

Allen's face was hard. "First, Meg's skiff is safe at the oil dock in Summerport. You can pick it up any time. I wanted you to know that I took it and that the kid is in no way to blame."

"You're one of the poachers," Meg's uncle said slowly. It was not a question, just a statement of facts.

"Why did you come back after you got away safely?" Meg wailed. She wanted to add, "Uncle Gilbert hates you. He'll be only too glad to turn you over to the warden."

Allen pulled one of her braids gently. "Hush, child. Yes, Mr. Duncan, I'm one of the poachers."

"Where's your companion?" asked Uncle Gilbert.

"Smalley Blake? I wouldn't know. We parted company in Summerport, when I decided to come back and face the music, rather than keep on the run for the rest of my life." There was a moment of silence, and then Allen went on. "I thought, too, that you'd blame Meg for losing the skiff. I'm too big to hide behind a kid."

Uncle Gilbert smiled faintly. "I almost did blame her."

Meg began to cry. "Have you got to go to jail?"

"There's no need to get worked up over it, Meg," Allen said quietly. "I'm on my way to see the sheriff now."

"I'll go with you," Uncle Gilbert said suddenly. "We can drive to town in the truck. Kit, go in and tell your mother that we won't be going to church this morning. No, Megan, go in with Kit. You can't come with us."

Meg sat brooding on the doorstep. Repulsive lay over her feet, kneading his claws into her sneakers. Kit had tried in vain to comfort her. "It was the best thing he could do, Meg. They'd be sure to catch him some time."

"It was that old Smalley Blake's fault. I wish he'd broken his neck!"

It wasn't going to help matters any that her Uncle Gilbert had gone into town with Allen, although the fact that he didn't like Allen would have little bearing on the case. However, Uncle Gilbert was so terribly honest and upright that

even if Allen had been his best friend, he wouldn't have let him go unpunished, Meg thought.

"Do you think he'll have to stay in jail for a very long time?" she asked finally.

Just then the truck drove into the dooryard. There were two people in it—Allen and Gilbert Duncan. Meg and Kit ran to meet them. "I thought you were in jail," said Meg.

Allen shook his head. "Not yet. The case will come up next week, and your uncle has gone bail for me."

Allen remained on the farm until it was time

for him to appear in court. Uncle Gilbert and Aunt Laura insisted that it was the only sensible thing for him to do, but in private Allen told his sister, "I bet he wants to keep an eye on me, now that he's put up all that money."

Although everyone treated Allen like a guest, he did chip in and try to help with the work, but it was clear that Allen had never been cut out to be a farmer. In spite of Kit's and Meg's instructions, he spilled mash, cracked eggs, and frightened the hens. "Darned feathered fools," he called them. But the dog, Heather, adored him; the black cat, Repulsive, came home every night and no longer tried to live up to his name; and Allen even taught Crow to say, "So what?"

Kit and Allen were soon good friends, and even Aunt Laura regarded him kindly and said she believed that his troubles had been caused by getting into bad company. Uncle Gilbert made no comment. He was polite to Allen, and Allen was polite to him, and that was all.

Meg was not as upset this time, when the day came for her brother to appear in court. Allen had told her that he would not go to jail after all. He would be fined, and Gilbert Duncan had agreed to pay the fine. "Then I'll earn the money and repay your uncle," Allen explained. He did have a few kind words to say about Uncle Gilbert. "He's not really a bad fellow, you know—just set in his ways."

Allen cleared his throat and then said, "You know, Meg, I may have stretched the facts a bit last fall in Summerport. That day I said your Uncle Gilbert had turned his back on your mother. The fact is, I'm not sure your mother and Dad ever tried to keep in touch with him. And I never let him know where you were or anything about you. So the truth of it is that he couldn't have helped you much, even if he'd wanted to."

Meg looked at her brother in surprise. "But I knew *that*," she said.

The fine was paid, and Allen was released, after a stiff warning from the judge. Old Red Carver turned his energy to hunting for Smalley Blake, although it wasn't likely Smalley would turn up in that part of the country again. Kit and Meg both assumed that the affair had come to a happy end. To repay the money borrowed from Gilbert Duncan, Allen would go to work on the farm, and the Duncans and the Elwells would live happily together ever after.

Of course it didn't turn out like that. Allen and Gilbert Duncan came to have a mutual respect for one another, but there would never be any affection between them. Allen was already sick of the farm. He could not wait to get back to the water. "With the herring starting to run this spring, I know where I can get a berth aboard a seiner." He had just dropped a bucket of eggs, cracking a half dozen of them, and Uncle Gilbert offered no objection to the plan.

"But Allen," Meg cried, "I thought you were going to stay with us."

"I'm like a fish on a hot griddle in this place," her brother answered. "Your uncle's a good man —too sober for my taste, but he's stood by me like a brother—and I'll say nothing against him. But I'd go crazy here."

Uncle Gilbert drove Allen into town to catch the bus for Summerport. There wasn't much room in the cab of the truck, but Meg was allowed to go along too. Kit and Aunt Laura said their good-by's at home, but after all, Meg was his sister.

Meg wore her new blue dress, with the blue socks, and blue-silk ribbons on her braids. She had grown an inch during the winter and now came up to Allen's shoulder. "You aren't a little girl any more," her brother said, and there was something a bit wistful in his voice.

But he was gay enough as he talked over his plans with Gilbert Duncan, while they waited for the bus to stop at the drugstore. "I'll make good money on this job, and I'll send you a check every month. No Elwell ever stayed in debt." He turned to Meg. "And when I get